The adventure so far . . .

Bailey Fish, eleven, was sent rather suddenly by her mother to live with her grandmother, Sugar, in Central Virginia. As Bailey adjusts to new surroundings, a father she has never known and her annoying half sister, Norma Jean, arrive unexpectedly and upset her. Bailey and her friends form the No Sisters Sisters Club to exclude Norma Jean. In time, as the sisters have scary adventures together, including helping catch someone trying to burn down an old house, they learn to get along to solve the mysteries. Then the boys arrive . . .

Also in the Bailey Fish Adventure Series

The Wild Women of Lake Anna
A finalist in *ForeWord* magazine's
2005 Book of the Year Contest

No Sisters Sisters Club

The Thief at Keswick Inn:

A Bailey Fish Adventure

Linda Salisbury
Drawings by
Christopher Grotke

Tabby House

Cover design: Lewis Agrell
Author photo: Ann Henderson
Illustrator photo: Paul Collins, courtesy of MuseArts

**Library of Congress Cataloging-in-Publication
Data**

Salisbury, Linda G. (Linda Grotke)
    The thief at Keswick Inn : a Bailey Fish adventure /
Linda Salisbury : drawings by Christopher Grotke.
       p.cm
Includes book club questions and related web sites.
Summary: When several items disappear from Keswick
Inn, eleven-year-old Bailey Fish and her new friends set a
trap to catch the culprit, but what they discover surprises
everyone.
    ISBN-13: 978-1881539-41-4
    [1. Friendship--Fiction. 2. Lost and found possessions--
Fiction. 3. Virginia--Fiction. 4. Mystery and detective
stories.] I. Grotke, Christopher A., ill. II. Title

PZ7.S1524Th 2006
[Fic]--dc22   2005046714

www.BaileyFishAdventures.com
http://BaileyFishAdventureBooks.blogspot.com

baileyfish@gmail.com

Classroom quantities available.

Tabby House
P.O. Box 544, Mineral, VA 23117
(540) 894-8868

Contents

1. New Neighbors — 7
2. Cleaning the Old House — 12
3. Mysterious Locket — 17
4. Double Fun — 20
5. A Buried Treasure — 26
6. Rocks and More Rocks — 30
7. Clover — 33
8. Sparkle Time — 38
9. Upstairs Room Five — 41
10. Work Crew Meeting — 44
11. Sad News — 47
12. E-mails from Far Away — 50
13. The Surprise — 54
14. Missing Money — 57
15. Bad News Family — 62
16. Visitors for Bailey — 65
17. Missing Locket — 68
18. First People — 72
19. Molly Arrives — 76

20. Bailey and the Bug Man   83
21. Gone Again   86
22. Hayseed Muckle   89
23. Another Discovery   96
24. The Triplets   100
25. More E-Mails   103
26. The Piano   106
27. Property for Sale   109
28. Sugar Calls a Meeting   111
29. Hard to Sleep   115
30. Meeting with Hadley Hudson   118
31. E-mail Surprises   123
32. One Mystery Solved   126
33. Powwow   130
34. Piano Lessons   136
35. Tending Sugar's Garden   139
36. Detective Books   143
37. Confrontation   147
38. The Thief   151
39. Fred's Plan   156
40. Apologies   160
41. Catching Dreams   166
Book Club Questions   169
Web Sites   173
From Sugar's Bookshelves   174
Glossary   175
Photos and Maps   178
Acknowledgments   187
About the Author   189
About the Illustrator   191

1

New Neighbors

"Ouch!" Bailey Fish said to her soft gray kitten. "You're too rough!"

Shadow blinked his wise yellow-gray eyes and waited for Bailey's hand to reach for him again. He grabbed it with his paws and licked her thumb before playfully biting down.

"Ow!" said Bailey. "You little rascal!"

Bailey reread the letter from her mother while she waited for her grandmother, Sugar, to get off the phone. Sugar said it was the perfect day to enlarge their vegetable garden that was in a sunny corner of the backyard. Soon they would plant lettuce, zucchinis, winter squash, pumpkins, tomatoes, parsley, peas, strawberries, and onions. Sugar said there was nothing like the taste of homegrown vegetables.

Bailey sighed, folded the letter from Costa Rica, and shoved it in her jeans pocket. She had been living in Central Virginia with her grandmother for months now and her mother showed no sign of returning to Florida, where she and Bailey had lived most of Bailey's eleven years. Instead, her mother's letters and e-mails were filled with excitement about the people she was interviewing for a magazine article and the wildlife she was seeing.

Bailey teased Shadow with her hand. He pounced on it.

"Hey," called a voice from the woods behind Sugar's house. Bailey looked up, startled. Two boys about her age dashed out of the path that led to an old graveyard and the rundown house beyond.

"Hey, yourself," she called back.

The boys came closer, tossing a small blue football between them. Shadow disappeared under a porch chair to watch them from safety.

The taller of the two said, "We're looking for Bailey."

"I'm Bailey."

"No way," said the shorter. "Isn't Bailey a boy?"

"No way," said Bailey. "I'm a girl."

The boys looked at each other and laughed.

"Well," said the taller, "when Dad told us to go find Bailey, we just figured Bailey was a boy."

"The joke's on us," said the shorter.

"Who's your dad?" asked Bailey.

"Will Keswick. He's fixing up the old Emmett farm. We're going to live there some day," said the older boy. "I'm Noah. He's Fred."

As Bailey studied them she saw that Noah resembled his dad. She had met their father a few months ago after an out-of-state developer and his men tried to burn down the old Emmett house and barn to force the Keswicks into selling the land. Noah had hair like his father's—the color of a yellow cat, and it stuck up every which way. She couldn't tell if he spiked it or if it were just naturally wild.

Fred didn't look at all like Noah. His hair was dark—the color of her grandmother's cast-iron frying pan—and curly. Noah had green eyes like Mr. Will, but Fred's were almost black, and he wore Harry Potter-style glasses perched on his turned-up nose. Noah's skin looked like he sunburned easily. Fred's was dark, as if deeply tanned. Fred's face was rounder than Noah's thin one. Each boy had a dimple in his chin and their father's friendly smile, but the boys did not look at all like brothers.

"Well, dude," said Noah, "are you coming to help us work at our house?"

"I need to ask Sugar. She wanted me to work in the vegetable garden today," said Bailey. "I'm sure she will say it's okay."

"We'll be here for the weekend," said Fred. "Maybe if you help us today, we can help you tomorrow. I'm sure Dad won't mind."

Fred wiped his glasses on his brown-and-green soccer jersey and peered through the lenses before putting them back on.

Bailey climbed the back steps two at a time, opened the creaky screen door, and went to Sugar's office. Her grandmother was hanging up the phone.

"Bailey, I hate to change our plans, but I really need to go to town to talk with a club about starting a roadside cleanup campaign. Their scheduled speaker is sick," Sugar said. "I've got to put on decent clothes and run."

"That's okay," said Bailey, grinning. "Mr. Will wants me to help him work on the house, and he sent Noah and Fred to get me."

"I haven't seen those boys in a few years, but they always struck me as lots of fun," said Sugar. "Sure, go ahead. And tell Will that I'll stop by when I'm done in town. I want to see how the work is coming."

Bailey called out the door to Noah and Fred, "I'll be ready in a minute."

She dashed up to her room, put her mother's letter in the top desk drawer, quickly brushed her medium-brown hair, grabbed her denim jacket, and hurried to the back porch where the boys were petting her kittens.

2

Cleaning the Old House

"Here, catch," said Noah as he tossed the football to Bailey. She almost fumbled but hung on, then threw it quickly to Fred. The boys looked surprised that she had handled the ball so well, especially because she hadn't expected them to throw it to her as she started across the backyard.

"Race you," said Fred, dashing for the path. The boys ran through the woods with Bailey close behind. She was glad she knew the way so well or she might have tripped over branches, or stepped in the little muddy creek.

"Beat you," said Fred, breathlessly, as they came into the clearing by the Emmett house.

"Wow! It looks better already," said Bailey, who was only slightly winded.

Since the last time she had seen the old house, shortly after the fire, it was obvious that the Keswicks had worked hard on the porches and yard. A pile of lumber replaced the boards that had been stored in a little barn when it was burned down. The yard between the house and the orchard was filled with building supplies and a small trailer for tools.

"Hey," called Mr. Will, from an upstairs window when he saw Bailey and his sons head toward the house. "Good to see you again. We're working up here."

"What are we doing?" asked Bailey.

"Cleaning out trash today," he said, "so we can really get going on the inside fix-up."

Noah and Fred led the way up the porch steps and into the house. The door was wide open to let in fresh air. Bailey remembered when she had first gone inside the abandoned house with Sugar. It was dark and spooky and they saw a nest of baby vultures in an upstairs bedroom. She didn't like the house at all then. Now it seemed different—friendly.

They found Mr. Will in the upstairs hall with brooms and large gray trash barrels.

"Bailey, I want you to meet my wife, Miss Bekka."

"My hands are dirty, so I can't give you a proper Keswick hello," said his wife, her brown eyes sparkling. "But we're glad you're able to help today." Her thick, dark-blond hair was pulled back in a single braid. Wispy strands curled around her face.

She handed Bailey a broom to sweep out the room where the vultures' nest had been while the boys carried trash from the corners and the attic.

Mr. Will made notes on a yellow pad as he measured the size of each room, and jotted down what had to be done. Some plaster walls needed patching before they could be painted; others needed to have woodwork replaced or repaired. His wife dipped a rag in a bucket of sudsy water as she washed the window ledges.

"It's been a long time since this house was cared for," Miss Bekka said to Bailey. "We can't wait to get the place fixed up so we can live here. Overall, it is in better condition than we had realized."

"It's bigger than I thought," said Bailey.

"I'll tell you a secret, said Miss Bekka. "We're thinking of turning it into a bed-and-breakfast for people who would like to spend a night or weekend in the country."

Bailey raised her eyebrows in surprise. She and her mother had stayed in a bed-and-breakfast near the ocean in Georgia when she was in third grade. She remembered how the owner bustled about to make the guests feel at home. She and her mom enjoyed the fresh blueberry muffins they had for breakfast before they rode their bikes along the path near the beach.

"I know it will be a lot of work," said Miss Bekka, "but I love company, and I have wonderful help."

It will be fun to have more people in the neighborhood, thought Bailey.

She was pleased with how clean the wooden floors looked in each room that she swept. Some rooms were empty, and others had dusty old furniture in them, such as dressers and bed frames. Will Keswick and the boys had already dragged moldy mattresses out to a pickup truck so they could take them and other trash to the landfill.

"Would you like me to dust the old furniture?" asked Bailey.

"That would be great," said Miss Bekka, handing her a clean rag. "Inside and out. We haven't opened all the drawers or explored all the closets."

Bailey started in a room that had a small dresser, a straight-back chair, and the headboard of a spindle bed.

She wiped the dresser top and the sides, then decided to look inside the drawers.

She found old photographs in one, blankets and pillowcases in another, and books in a third. In a small drawer at the top, something wrapped in a thin, pink cloth sack had slipped into a crack at the back. Bailey put down her cleaning rag and opened the sack.

"Miss Bekka, Miss Bekka, look what I found!" cried Bailey, her hazel eyes shining. "Come quick!"

3

Mysterious Locket

When the Keswicks heard Bailey call, they hurried into the room.

"What is it?" asked Miss Bekka, worried that Bailey might have hurt herself on a rusty nail or piece of broken glass.

"Look what was in this drawer!" said Bailey. She held out a heavy silver necklace with a large oval locket attached.

"Oh, my," said Miss Bekka. "I had no idea such valuables were left behind."

Bailey handed it to her. The boys' mother looked at the fancy engraving, then carefully opened the locket. There were two pictures inside it. One was of a man wearing a dark cap, a striped shirt, and suspenders. He had a long mustache that tipped up at the ends so that he looked like he had a W glued under his nose. The other was of a beautiful young woman with a mound of hair twisted in a bun on top of her head. Her starched white dress had a high lace collar and tiny buttons down to her waist.

"Who is it?" asked Bailey. "Is it Mr. Emmett and his cousin, Miss Dolly—the one who played the piano for him and painted pictures?"

"I don't think so," said Miss Bekka, handing the locket to her husband.

"Let me see, Dad," said Noah.

"There's an inscription," said their father. *"From E.G.E. to M.M.P."*

"That could be Cousin Edgar," said Miss Bekka. "Weren't those his initials? Edgar George Emmett? But M.M.P.? That's a mystery. We need to put this in a safe place," she said. "It might be a family treasure."

Bailey said, "Maybe there are clues in the dresser or other boxes in the house. There are lots of letters and stuff in the drawers."

"I guess we shouldn't throw out anything until we go through everything very carefully," said Will Keswick.

"I'll help, and so will Sugar. She likes antiques," said Bailey. "You should see her attic!"

"I did, a long time ago," said Mr. Will. "It was a little scary." His green eyes twinkled. "I have an idea. Let's create a sorting area in the third upstairs bedroom. I have sawhorses and doors that we can make into tables."

Fred helped Bailey take the books, pictures, and papers from the drawers into the sorting room while Noah helped his father carry the doors up the stairs.

"Wow!" said Bailey, as she spread the photos out. "Here's another picture of the woman in the locket. She's holding a little book." Bailey studied the picture closely. "I can't make out what it says on the cover."

"I can't read it, either," said Fred, as he examined the picture.

"I hate to break up this party," said Miss Bekka, "but I'd like to finish the basic cleaning before lunch." She smiled as she retied a yellow scarf around her hair.

"I have one more room to sweep," said Bailey, "and the hall." She picked up the broom where she had dropped it.

"Anyone home?" called a voice from downstairs.

"Hey, Sugar's here," said Bailey.

4

Double Fun

"I figured you hard workers might be hungry, so I picked up fried chicken at the general store," said Sugar, as she put a large white sack on the kitchen table.

"That's great," said Bekka Keswick. "I was just going to make tuna sandwiches, but chicken sounds like a nice treat. How was your meeting?"

"Good," said Sugar, as she looked down the hallway toward the living room. "We are planning to try to embarrass those who litter by putting up roadside signs that say things like REAL MEN DON'T LITTER, or ONLY SLOBS LITTER. I hope we get their attention."

She walked down the hall. "This sure looks a lot better than the last time we were in here just after the fire," said Sugar. "You have already done a lot."

"They are going to make it into a bed-and-breakfast," said Bailey. "Oops, that was supposed to be a secret." She looked at Miss Bekka.

"It's okay to tell Sugar. We haven't announced that officially," said Mr. Will, "but we have plenty of extra bedrooms for guests. Bekka is a wonderful cook, and we think it would be grand for the boys to grow up in the country."

"A perfect spot and a perfect use for an old house," said Sugar.

"Mr. Will said he will pay me, Fred, and Noah, if we work on the house and yard," said Bailey.

"Not too much money, now," Sugar said to Will. "I don't want her to stop helping me for free!" Sugar's face crinkled into a giant smile. "We have a garden to dig and plant, and I need my favorite helper around the house."

"Don't worry, Sugar," said Bailey. She was already thinking about how much fun it would be to help the Keswicks.

Miss Bekka said, "Come with me, Sugar. I want your opinion about what to do with the kitchen cupboards and floor."

While the women talked, Bailey finished sweeping the sixth upstairs room. It had a large trunk in the corner, so heavy that it took both boys to drag it into the sorting room. The lock was rusted closed. "I'll get oil from Dad's toolbox," said Fred. "There might be other treasures inside."

"What are you going to use your pay for?" Noah asked Bailey.

"I dunno. Maybe a plane ticket to Costa Rica."

"What's there?"

"My mom. She's a wild woman off on an adventure. She's writing an article for a big magazine."

"A wild woman? What's a wild woman?" asked Fred, sitting on the trunk.

"Those are the women in our family who do wild things. They travel and lead interesting lives. One was a spy. Another, a long time ago, traveled around the country dressed up as a man. Another lived with chimpanzees for three years and then wrote a book about them," said Bailey, proudly.

"That's way cool. Is that why you live with Sugar?" asked Noah.

"Yeah, for a while anyway. What are you going to save for?"

Fred thought for a minute, then said, "A new dirt bike. Mine is rusty and messed up. It's really old."

Noah said, "I want a camcorder so I can make movies."

"What kind of movies?" asked Bailey.

"Documentaries. I'll write the scripts and you and Fred can be in them."

"Really!" said Bailey. "Me, a Hollywood movie star." She stuck her nose in the air and walked slowly around the room with her hands on her hips.

"Do you miss your mom?" asked Noah. He pretended he was filming her.

"Yeah." Bailey wasn't sure how much more she wanted to tell them so she decided to change the subject. "How come you guys don't look alike?" she blurted out.

Noah and Fred looked at each other and laughed.

"We're both twelve," said Fred. "Maybe we're twins."

Twins? That couldn't be. She was puzzled as she studied their faces.

"Okay, dude, I'll tell you. Fred's adopted," said Noah.

"So is Noah," said Fred.

Now Bailey was really confused. "But you look like Mr. Will," she said to Noah.

"He's really my uncle. My birth parents died in a car wreck when I was just a baby. Uncle

Will and Aunt Bekka took me in and became my parents."

"And they had already applied to adopt me," said Fred.

"What happened to your birth parents?" Bailey asked Fred.

"He's from Jamaica and she was born in South Carolina. That's all I know. I was almost one when I was adopted."

Noah asked Bailey, "Do you have brothers or sisters?"

"I just found out that I have a father, a half sister, and two half brothers," she said. "They live in Guam, but might be moving closer. Norma Jean—she's ten—doesn't really look like me, either." Bailey thought about how her father and Norma Jean had just showed up one day. "Do you think your parents—the ones who had you—will ever come looking for you?" she asked Fred.

He wiped his glasses again. "Even if they do, Mom and Dad are my real parents."

"But do you want to meet your birth parents?" asked Bailey. She surprised herself by being so nosy.

"I don't know," said Fred. "Mom and Dad always say they would help me find them if I want to, but right now I don't want to."

"We'd better get finished," said Noah impatiently, "or we won't get paid."

"Come for lunch," they heard Sugar call a few minutes later.

The brothers bolted for the stairs, playfully pounding each other. Bailey leaned the broom against the wall and quickly followed, not turning around to pick it up when she heard it fall. She was enjoying having the "twins" as neighbors.

5

A Buried Treasure

"What's this afternoon's project?" Sugar asked, as she put the paper plates and chicken bones in the garbage can.

Will told her he wanted to get bushes trimmed and part of the yard raked. "Then tomorrow, we'll give you a hand spading and hoeing your vegetable garden before we head back to Arlington."

"I'm pretty good with clippers," said Sugar, "and Bailey is great with a rake. And we will be grateful to have help digging in that soil! It's as hard as a flowerpot."

"I'll be glad when we'll be staying here for more than just weekends," said Miss Bekka. "This place is so peaceful."

"I want you guys to help me drag branches to the burn pile," said Mr. Will to the work crew, "and then we'll dig up that small boxwood. I want to move it closer to the house where we can enjoy its fragrance."

Bailey put on a pair of brown cotton gloves so she wouldn't get blisters and began raking leaves and twigs out of an old flower bed near the front steps. She could hear Sugar's clippers and Miss Bekka's broom.

Noah and Fred made her laugh every time they came past her carrying large branches. One time they pretended they were riding stick horses. Another time they acted like the branches were so heavy that they could barely carry them.

Once the boys pretended like they were rowing a boat. On the next trip, they came by without carrying any branches and just did handstands before they ran off laughing.

Bailey filled bushel basket after bushel basket with leaves and took them to an area where Mr. Will said he was going to create a compost pile. He said he would use the decayed material next year in his garden.

Mr. Will asked if Bailey would dig a hole for the boxwood. She soon discovered the dirt was full of small rocks—so many that Mr. Will finally took the shovel and helped her finish.

"Save the larger stones," he said, "and we'll make a rock garden around the big tulip tree."

As Bailey pulled stones from the bottom of the hole, she felt something that was oddly shaped for a rock. It was flat and had sharp edges. She pulled it out and held it in her palm.

"A small arrowhead. It's called a projectile point," said Mr. Will. He called to the boys to see it. "There were several tribes in this region. We'll have to do research to learn about them."

"Cool," said Noah. "Maybe we will find more." He took the shovel. "What is an arrowhead doing near the house?"

"Remember," said his father, "the Native Americans were here long before the European settlers arrived and built houses. I heard there have been a number of Indian artifacts found near Bear Castle just down the road, and all over the county."

"Bear Castle?" said Bailey. "That's a funny name."

Sugar explained, "Thomas Jefferson's brother-in-law, Dabney Carr, was born there. The old house is now in the middle of a modern subdivision near the lake, which wasn't here when the house was built."

Bailey looked at the flaked edges of the arrowhead. She wondered if she should keep it or give it to the Keswicks.

"I think you should have this," said Bailey. "It was from your yard. I might find another in mine when we plant our garden."

"That's generous of you," said Mr. Will. "I know the boys will treasure it."

Fred said, "Maybe we can put it in a glass case and make a sign that says DISCOVERED BY BAILEY FISH."

Bailey smiled. She wished it were summer vacation so that the boys would be around all the time.

6

Rocks and More Rocks

"As you know from helping the Keswicks, this digging is harder than it looks," said Sugar. "The soil here is difficult to work with. Look at all the stones I've already pulled out of this little patch of garden." She pointed at a pile of rocks that were the size of eggs, apples, and potatoes, and handed Bailey green cotton work gloves and a trowel.

Bailey put down the book she had been reading and put on the gloves.

"Mr. Will and the boys were a great help clearing this spot to enlarge the garden, but now the tough part begins," said Sugar.

Bailey rolled up the sleeves on her favorite purple sweatshirt that her mother had given her for Christmas. She was afraid that she was outgrowing it because the sleeves no longer covered her wrists. As Bailey worked the trowel down a few inches, she constantly hit rocks that she had to remove. She tossed them in a cardboard box that Sugar had placed between them.

Bailey remembered how easy it was to dig in the sandy Florida soil. But the little garden that she and her mother planted two winters ago in Port Charlotte hadn't done very well. Something ate the roots of the tomatoes, rabbits got into the lettuce, and Bailey and her mom were bitten by nasty fire ants while they weeded.

"In Florida we planted our garden in the fall, not the spring," Bailey said. "It was too hot for the plants to grow in the summer. We had lots of grapefruit and oranges in the winter."

"I remember that box of fruit you sent me last January," said Sugar. "Delicious." She stood up and stretched. "I see that you have decided to read *The Secret Garden*. It is one of my favorite childhood books."

"Emily said it is good," said Bailey. "I've just started, so I don't know about the secret part yet."

Sugar rested for a moment while she surveyed their progress. "Gardening, and being outside in nature, are good for all of us, just like you'll read in that book. I can't wait to hear what you think about the story. In fact, when you discover your favorite part, I want you to read that chapter to me."

Bailey said, "Okay. When do you think we'll plant the vegetables?"

Sugar said, "Soon. The weather is warming and the danger of frost is almost past. Frost isn't something you had very often in Florida, is it?"

"Not where we lived," said Bailey, "but sometimes in January it got pretty cold. We always wore our jackets, but people visiting were trying to get a suntan, so they looked silly in their shorts."

"Including me that time I came to see you when you were in kindergarten. Remember?"

Bailey laughed. "Not really."

The setting sun glowed bright red through the trees, its rays streaming like shimmering strings of light.

Sugar said, "Time to go in so we don't look like silly tourists from Florida who don't know when to get warm when the air is chilly."

"You're funny," said Bailey, as she knocked the dirt off her trowel before putting the tool in Sugar's wheelbarrow.

7

Clover

"Yo, Bailey," shouted Noah. "Come with me right now! We've got something neat to show you."

Bailey looked at Sugar, who said, "Run on over. I can finish hanging the rest of this laundry by myself."

Noah had already vanished down the path and Bailey had to run hard to catch up.

She tried to guess what the surprise might be. The Keswicks were back for the weekend. Maybe they had found something else in the attic or had finished painting a room. Maybe the electricity was finally turned on.

Dang, Bailey thought as her shoelace came loose. She had to stop running to retie it.

When she reached the old house she saw Noah and Fred huddled over something on the front porch. Fred held it up.

"Sweet," said Bailey, as a whiskery white-and-tan face tried to lick her.

"We got her at the shelter," said Fred, with a big grin. "Want to hold her?"

He placed the wiggly pup in Bailey's arms. The dog was shaggy. Her body was longer than she was tall and she had ears that moved around like sails. Long strands of fur hung from them.

"This is the weirdest-looking dog I've ever seen," said Bailey. The soft puppy licked her face and squealed with joy.

"That's one reason we picked her," said Fred.

"Actually, she picked us," said Noah.

"What's her name?" asked Bailey.

"We've been trying to think of a good one," said Fred. "I liked Spot, Betsy, Frieda, or Virginia."

"I want to call her Speedy or Rover because she runs around like crazy," said Noah.

"That's no name for a girl," said Bailey. "You should call her Clover. She's white and looks like the top of a clover."

The boys smiled at each other.

"Excellent," said Noah.

"Agreed," said Fred. "Okay, Clover, fetch."

He threw a stick into the yard. Clover ran until she stumbled and fell over. She picked up the stick and ran in a circle.

"See?" said Fred.

"You have to call her," said Bailey. "Here, girl. Here, Clover." Clover looked at Bailey and lay down in the grass with the stick in her mouth. She wanted to be chased. Bailey stood up and walked slowly toward the dog. When Bailey got within three feet, Clover gave a cheerful growl, grabbed the stick and raced around in circles. This time, the boys raced with her. She outran them easily.

Suddenly an ugly brown dog with ragged ears came out of nowhere, ran after Clover, and pinned her to the ground. Clover yelped.

"Stop," screamed Bailey, as she ran toward the dogs. The brown dog didn't move. The hair on its neck stood up like horns on a dragon.

"Ninja, come back," shouted a voice from the driveway.

Ninja stepped back, then trotted over to a boy on a bike.

"Are you okay, girl?" asked Noah. He rubbed Clover's belly. Instead of being afraid, she looked like she wanted to play with the dog.

"Who's that?" asked Noah.

"Justin," Bailey said. "He goes to my school."

"He better not let his dog hurt Clover," warned Noah.

"Hey," said Justin. "Ninja didn't mean to scare your dog. I didn't know you had one."

Noah folded his arms across his chest. "You live around here?"

"Down the road," said Justin. "You moving here?"

"Yeah," said Fred, "as soon as it's fixed up."

Bailey watched their faces. Fred seemed glad to meet Justin, but Noah was scowling.

Justin shifted on his feet, like he wasn't sure what Bailey had told the boys about him. He had been mean to her when she first arrived at Sugar's house. He had called her "Florida girl," and had made fun of her name. Justin didn't know if Bailey still thought he was still a mean dork.

She remembered how nervous Justin had made her feel the first time they met, but he had been friendlier lately. She simply said, "Noah and Fred will be riding on the bus with us next year, when their house gets done."

Fred put Clover back on the ground, and she immediately dashed over to see Ninja; his hair stood up on his neck again.

"Easy, boy," said Justin.

The two dogs sniffed each other. Clover put her front legs flat on the ground like she was bowing, then jumped straight in the air and ran in a big circle. Ninja watched, like Clover was nuts. He had forgotten that he had been a puppy. During her final circle, Clover ran to the larger dog and flopped on the ground, panting hard. Ninja looked bored, but his tail wagged a little.

"I guess they will be okay," said Fred.

Just then their father came out of the house. "Ahh, another helper has shown up. Hi, I'm Will Keswick. And you are?"

"Justin Rudd." The short boy with dark hair and faded orange T-shirt took off his baseball cap and held out his hand. "Your helper?" Justin was surprised.

"I'm serious," said their dad. "If you want to earn some extra money, we can use all the hands we can get on this place."

Justin stammered, "I gotta tell my mom. Gee, thanks. C'mon, Ninja." He whistled for the brown dog as he ran for his bike.

"Dad," said Noah, "you don't even know him."

"I know enough," said Mr. Will.

8

Sparkle Time

As Justin pedaled quickly down the driveway with Ninja racing behind him, Mr. Will went back inside. Bailey, Fred, and Noah looked at each other in silence.

"Dad's always doing stuff like that," Noah said. "He gives people jobs all the time, but I don't know about Justin. He looks . . . "

"Justin seems okay," said Fred.

Bailey decided not to say anything. She wasn't sure if she liked Justin either, but he had been nicer since she was helping his little sister, Fern, learn to read. Bailey knelt down and rubbed Clover's moppy head.

"I need good workers up here," called Miss Bekka, "and you three people are just the ones!"

Clover grabbed Bailey's cotton work glove and raced away. "Hey," said Bailey, chasing after the merry little dog. "I need that."

"We've got more in the house. Maybe if we ignore her, she'll bring it back," said Fred. "Mom's waiting."

Bailey decided that he was right and followed the boys into the house. But Fred wasn't right. Clover lay down under a lilac bush and chewed the glove, shaking it frequently.

Every time Bailey went inside the old house, she was astonished by its size and the number of rooms that opened from long halls. Miss Bekka had set out paper towels and spray bottles with window cleaner for each of them.

"It's sparkle time. We'll start with inside windows today. No streaks or smudges, please," she said.

Noah turned on a battery-operated radio and tried to find music. The strongest signal came from a country station in Fredericksburg.

Bailey sprayed the windowpanes. She could see Clover digging. "I think she's burying my glove," she said to the boys.

"Wow! Look at her go," said Fred. Dirt was flying everywhere and the little white dog was covered with it. "Mom won't let her in the van like that. We may need to give her a bath before we go home."

"That's one good thing about cats," said Bailey. "They don't get very dirty, except when they walk in the mud or get covered with spiderwebs. That's what Mom always says."

"So, when will you see your mom again?" asked Noah.

"I dunno. Maybe this summer. She might come back for a visit. She's very busy right now."

"What about your dad?" asked Fred.

"He didn't say when they'd be back."

"Hmm," said Noah. "I don't remember my birth parents, and Fred doesn't remember his, but it doesn't matter because we're family now. Right, bro?"

Fred gave him a high-five.

"I see a streak on your window," said Bailey, pointing to the one Noah was working on.

"It's on the outside," said the boy. "Dad will have to reach it on a tall ladder."

Bailey took the cleaner and sprayed the next window. *Norma Jean will like the boys,* she thought.

9

Upstairs Room Five

"By the way, we won't be riding the bus to school," said Fred.

"How come?" asked Bailey. "Aren't you moving here?"

"Upstairs room number five is our school," said Noah.

"Huh?" said Bailey, figuring the twins were just goofing around again.

"Really," said Fred. "We're homeschooled. Mom is our teacher."

Bailey pushed her hair back behind her ears, then put her hands in her pockets. She had never met kids who had all their lessons taught at home.

"I don't get it," she said. "Do you do the same work as regular kids?"

"We're regular, dude," said Noah, playfully sticking out his tongue at her. "And yes, we do the same work—maybe even more—because we go at our own pace. And Fred and I go at a very fast pace."

"Don't you get lonely?" asked Bailey.

"Naw," said Fred. "We get together with other homeschoolers for field trips, sports, and music. Stuff like that."

"When do you go to school?"

"We have a schedule for our classes, but the neat thing is," said Noah, "if we want to take a trip, we can do our schoolwork in the van, or do a special project and catch up on the weekend. School is always in session."

"Wait till you see our school," said Fred. "We have desks, a work table, science equipment, computers, bookshelves, and art supplies."

"And our teacher is really tough," interrupted Noah. "No messing around. She has to do her homework, too, to be prepared every day for our lessons."

"And when Dad isn't working, he quizzes us on what we've studied. He wants to see if we've thought about what we've learned, not just memorized it," added Fred.

"I've always gone to regular school," said Bailey, wishing the boys were going to ride her bus and attend her school so they could meet all her friends.

"Regular school?" Noah crossed his eyes at her.

"I mean public school," said Bailey. "And I like it a lot."

"I bet we read more books," said Noah.

"Bet I do," said Bailey, sticking out her tongue at him.

"And we're learning Latin and Spanish," said Fred.

"What's happened to my crew?" called Mr. Will. "It's time to get to work."

"Betcha we're better at spelling," said Noah, giving Bailey's hair a tug as he grabbed the sandpaper.

"Nuh-uh," said Bailey, with a big smile. "And Sugar and I are going to learn more about the Indians than you are. So there!"

"Ha!" said Fred, as he hurried off in the direction of his father.

10

Work Crew Meeting

Justin dropped his bike on the lawn and told Ninja to lie down and stay. The dog sighed and did as he was commanded. Clover napped in the hole under the lilac bush, exhausted from her morning adventures.

Will Keswick called Noah, Fred, Bailey, and Justin together for what he called a "work crew meeting." He pulled a notebook out of a pile of papers on a small round table.

"We have an honor system here at Keswick Inn," he said. "Each of you will have a section in the book in which to write down what work you did and how long it took. Every two weeks, I will add up the hours and pay you in cash. I'll be checking to make sure that jobs are done right, so don't take any shortcuts. Any questions?"

Bailey said, "Keswick Inn? I thought you called this the Emmett House?"

"Take a look at the sign I just painted," said Mr. Will. "I think a fixed-up house needs a new name."

Bailey hadn't noticed the sign. It wasn't painted very well, but the red letters did show up on the white board that was leaning next to the front porch. *Norma Jean would do a better job*, thought Bailey. *Maybe she can paint a nice one when she comes back.*

"Today, we'll scrub down the bathrooms," said Mr. Will.

"Oh, yuck!" said Noah.

"No scrub, no pay," said his dad. "We are hoping to get the electricity turned on this week so that the pump will work. Then, once we get the county permits, we can actually stay in the house instead of in the camper trailer."

Noah and Bailey carried gallons of bottled water to the downstairs bathroom while Fred and Justin worked upstairs.

Noah said, "This is girls' work."

"No way," said Bailey, and threw a soapy sponge at him.

Noah laughed and splashed water on her.

"Look at the mess you've made on the floor," she said.

"The better to scrub with," said Noah. "Hey, Bailey, any cute girls in your school?"

"I'm not telling," said Bailey. Her heart sank. Maybe the twins would like other girls, like her friend, Emily, better than her once they met them. Everybody thought Emily was cute with her dark, curly hair and constant, perky smile.

Fred peeked in. "We're done, and you aren't even half finished," he said.

After Justin had completed his tasks, he wrote down his time in the book, then left without saying a word.

"What's with him?" asked Noah, with a scowl.

11

Sad News

Bailey rocked in her purple chair while she waited for Sugar to make a shopping list. She was halfway through Sugar's copy of *The Secret Garden*. The orphaned Mistress Mary had just met her guardian, Mr. Craven, after living in his mansion for several months. He'd asked if she wanted toys or books or dolls. But Mary, who had discovered the secret garden and was tending it, said:

"Might I," quavered Mary, "might I have a bit of earth?"

"Earth!" he repeated. "What to you mean?"

"To plant seeds in—to make things grow—to see them come alive," Mary faltered.

That's crazy, thought Bailey. *I'd take books over dirt.* Even so, she really enjoyed reading about Mary's change from a spoiled brat to a fun kid who liked nature.

Bailey heard the phone ring. *I hope Sugar doesn't talk long*, she thought. *It's time to leave.*

Sugar came out without her car keys and sat in her rocker. "That call was from Will," she said. "His grandmother, Miss Dolly, has died. Very peacefully." Sugar sighed. "Nurse Karen told him that Miss Dolly had a good week. She had looked at family albums and her artwork and wanted to sit where she could listen to her favorite music and watch the yellow finches at her thistle feeders."

Bailey put her book down. She didn't remember anyone who had died except her cat Barker. He had been hit by a car just after Christmas when she was living in Florida. She and her mother buried him with his favorite mouse toys in the backyard. Bailey had said a prayer and had made a little cross out of sticks. Both she and her mother had hugged each other and cried and cried as they remembered all the silly things that Barker had done. She had loved Barker almost as much as she loved her mom.

"Guess we'd better get our shopping done. Will said he'd call back about the funeral arrangements," Sugar said. "I'll get my list and keys."

"I'm glad I got to know Miss Dolly a little," said Bailey, after they climbed into Sugar's red pickup. Miss Dolly had scared her when Bailey and Norma Jean had met her in the woods in late winter where the old woman had been lost for several days. Miss Dolly had kidnapped Bailey's kitten because she thought it was Bootsie, her own childhood cat. Later, Bailey and Norma Jean had gone to see Miss Dolly when she was having one of her good days, and they discovered that she had been an artist and musician.

"I was proud of you and Norma Jean for visiting Miss Dolly after she snatched Sallie. You had every right to be afraid of her," said Sugar.

"She said I had the right kind of fingers to play the piano," said Bailey.

"And that's one of the things we are going to look for on our adventures this spring," said Sugar. "A piano and a teacher."

12

E-mails from Far Away

Sugar and Bailey returned from the funeral home where they had attended Miss Dolly's calling hours. They had signed their names in a guest book and talked to the Keswicks and the neighbors. They were given a little shiny card with the dates of Miss Dolly's birth and death, a picture of a rose, and the words of the Twenty-third Psalm printed on it. Bailey put the card in her desk drawer, then decided to check her e-mail.

She hadn't heard from Norma Jean or their father since they had returned to Guam. She knew that her half sister would be sad that Miss Dolly had died because they both liked art.

People at the calling hours said that Miss Dolly had "passed on," or had "crossed the river." Bailey knew that they meant Miss Dolly had just plain died and gone to heaven.

It was the first time Bailey had met Martha Keswick, Mr. Will's mother. She noticed that Martha Keswick looked a lot like Miss Dolly. Martha Keswick said she had a surprise for Bailey, something that she would tell her about a few days after the funeral.

Bailey couldn't imagine what it might be, and Sugar acted as if she didn't know either. But Sugar's lips were twitching, like she was trying to keep from smiling, so Bailey was suspicious that her grandmother knew about the surprise.

Bailey e-mailed Norma Jean:

From: "Bailey"<baileyfish@gmail.com>
To: <pjfish2005@yermail.net>
Sent: 7:40 p.m.
Subject: Hi

I saw Miss Dolly's casket during the calling hours. It was closed so I didn't see her face. There were lots of flowers and a photo of her when she was very young and pretty. Her daughter brought the picture you drew of her and put it where everyone could see it. Noah and Fred had to dress up. The preacher said a prayer. People didn't cry because Miss Dolly was so old, except for Nurse Karen. Bailey.

At the end she typed SCR for Sisters Club Rocks. It was something she, Emily, Amber, and Heather had agreed to do once they had stopped the No Sisters Sisters Club, which was for best friends only, and had formed the Sisters Club for best friends *and* sisters.

She saw that there was an e-mail from Amber, her best friend in Florida.

From: <jbs25@yermail.net>
To: "Bailey"<Baileyfish@gmail.com>
Sent: 4:15 p.m.
Subject: Dance

Guess what? Benjie Price just asked me to go to the fifth-grade dinner dance. We're not supposed to have dates, but I can meet him there. I got a new yellow dress and white shoes at the mall. Do you have dances at your school? It is hot here. Have you heard from NJ? SCR. Amber.

To Amber:

From: "Bailey"<Baileyfish@gmail.com>
To: <jbs25@yermail.net>
Sent: 7:50 p.m.
Subject: Norma Jean

Haven't heard from NJ. I think she's in Guam now. I don't know what we do at the end of school. Maybe there will be a party. Justin is helping the Keswicks. Noah doesn't trust him, but I don't know why because Justin has been OK lately. He hasn't been mean to me or anyone. Gotta go. Sugar wants to use the computer. SCR. Bailey

Sugar said, "Oh, my, look at the time. You need to get to bed, and I have research to do on the Internet. I want to learn more about that projectile point you found and the tribes that hunted or lived in this area."

"Mr. Will thinks it might be from the Rappahannocks or the Pamunkeys," said Bailey.

"Could be, but we don't know for sure. Give me a kiss and off to bed."

13

The Surprise

"Well, here she is, that charming granddaughter of yours," said Martha Keswick as Bailey came home from school three days after Miss Dolly's funeral. Bailey put her book bag on the round hall table, took off her sneakers, and said hi.

Bailey didn't know if she should ask about the surprise, so she just pulled up a chair at the kitchen table and smiled. Sugar and Mrs. Keswick were finishing their mugs of peppermint tea, Sugar's favorite afternoon drink on a cool spring day.

"How was school?" asked Sugar.

"Good. I got an A on my math quiz and an A plus in band. And, I played my scales without any mistakes."

"Math and music ability often go together," said Mrs. Keswick. "They both require counting and dividing. And that brings me to why I stopped by."

Bailey leaned forward with great interest.

"Now, this wasn't officially in my mother's will, but she told me it is what she wanted done. That's good enough for me," said Mrs. Keswick.

What? What is it? Bailey couldn't stand the suspense.

Martha Keswick leaned forward and took one of Bailey's hands in hers. "Miss Dolly told me you have good hands for playing the piano, and she wanted you to have her old Boardman & Gray upright after she died. Will and the boys don't need it because they have Uncle Emmett's. And I certainly don't need another thing in my itty-bitty, overcrowded house. So, if you would like the piano, it is yours." Mrs. Keswick beamed as she waited for Bailey's response.

Bailey was so surprised that she was quiet for a moment, then said, "Really? For me? That's awesome. Thank you, Mrs. Keswick."

She looked at Sugar. Her grandmother smiled and said to Martha Keswick, "I've already figured out where we can put it. There is space in the parlor, the room we use as a library, if we rearrange the furniture."

"As you know, my mother was a fine musician, artist, and teacher. She recognized that you have potential," said Mrs. Keswick. "I'm just sorry that she couldn't have lived long enough to see you play the piano."

Bailey's cheeks reddened. She felt bad that she had not spent more time at Miss Dolly's house getting to know the old woman.

"Thank you," said Bailey. "I'll practice hard. And I'll take good care of it. I promise."

"Grand," said Mrs. Keswick. "I'll arrange for a piano mover to get it over here."

14

Missing Money

The Keswicks stayed at Miss Dolly's house for the rest of the week following the funeral. They cleaned Miss Dolly's house in the morning, then worked at Keswick Inn in the afternoon. Both Bailey and Justin went over each day as soon as they changed out of their school clothes.

One afternoon, Justin nodded to Will and Fred, then signed his name and the time in the notebook. He went upstairs to help Mr. Will pull badly damaged plaster off the wall in a front bedroom that looked out into a large branch of the huge tulip tree.

"Why doesn't Justin ever say anything," grumbled Noah. He was complaining more and more about Justin, finding fault with everything he did or didn't do. Fred and Bailey looked at each other and signed their names in the book before sanding the baseboards and doors in the hall and dining room.

Miss Bekka carefully covered Mr. Emmett's piano with a sheet so the dust from sanding would not get into it.

"Anybody home?"

"In here, Sugar," Bailey called.

Sugar carried a large cardboard box filled with old newspapers. Clover, with a dish towel in her mouth, trailed behind her, wagging her tail and jumping around Sugar's feet. "I figured you'd need these when we paint. Even if the floors will be refinished later, there is no point getting them splattered now," said Sugar. She placed the box in the center of the living room. Clover sniffed it inside and out.

"Those papers aren't for you," said Fred. "You're supposed to be housebroken now." He scratched Clover's head and she rolled on her back, licking his hand like it was candy.

"Mr. Will said we can help with the undercoat," Bailey said to her grandmother. "He wants to do the final coat himself so it will be perfect."

Just then they heard Mr. Will yell, "Take a look at this, crew!"

They dropped their sandpaper and hurried up the stairs, with Sugar and Clover behind them.

Mr. Will and Justin were examining an old sock. Mr. Will whistled in amazement. "Just look at this! Justin found it inside the wall when we were knocking out the plaster."

The man's tan sock, tied closed with a black shoelace, was heavy. As Mr. Will opened the top and tipped it over, coins spilled into his hand and onto the floor. Justin bent down and picked up three that were near his feet. He studied them carefully before handing them back to Mr. Will.

"This house is full of surprises," said Sugar. "Let me see them." She examined the coins closely and said, "Sure looks like real money to me. Perhaps someone put the sock in there during the Depression. The banks weren't a safe place at that time so people, like my mother, hid money inside mattresses or walls, or even under floorboards."

"How much is there, Dad?" asked Noah.

"We'll count it later. But for now, let's put it in the sorting area," said Mr. Will. He handed the sock to Fred.

Noah watched Justin's face as Fred left the room. "He looks like he wishes Dad had given him the sock to keep," muttered Noah to Bailey, "but it belongs to Keswick Inn, just like the arrowhead you found."

"Back to work, you guys," said Mr. Will. He and Justin picked up chunks of plaster, while the rest of the crew returned to sanding, and Sugar headed for the kitchen. Clover barked.

"Somebody needs to start training that dog," said Miss Bekka. "She chewed the rungs on the kitchen stool and scratched wallpaper in the back hall. If I had realized she was going to be so much trouble, I'd have insisted that we adopt the old poodle that was asleep in its cage next to her."

"Sure, Mom. I'll train her to help paint," said Noah, offering a brush to Clover. She wagged her tail happily.

"Back to work," said his mother, with a laugh.

Shortly after five o'clock, Justin signed out, again without saying anything to Fred, Noah, or Bailey, and rode away on his rusty bike. Ninja trotted behind him.

"It's almost time for supper," said Mr. Will. "I think we've done enough for one day."

"Can we count the money now?" asked Noah.

"Sounds like a plan," said his father.

Fred got to the sorting area first. His eyebrows furrowed in puzzlement. He looked under the low table where he had put the sock, then moved the teapot, necklace, arrowhead, and bed linens that they had found.

"Dad, I don't know what happened to it," said Fred. "I know I put it on the table."

"Are you sure?" asked his father, moving boxes as he searched.

Bailey heard Noah mutter to Fred, "I bet I know who took it. Justin was in a real hurry to leave today."

Fred whispered, "You better not say anything to Dad unless you have proof. You know how he is."

"I'll get proof!" hissed Noah.

15

Bad News Family

When Bailey returned the following afternoon, Justin wasn't there yet. Noah and Fred were spreading newspapers around the edges of the living room. She signed her time in the log book and pushed up her sweatshirt sleeves.

"Dad said we could put a primer coat on the baseboards today," said Fred. "He'll be back soon to show us what to do."

Clover dashed into the room, skidding before she reached the center. She was getting bigger by the day. Noah had taught her several tricks, which she did when she was in the mood, especially if he had a treat for her.

"Roll over, Clover," Noah said. Clover barked and sat up. "That's not rolling over, you goofball." Clover barked again, then rolled over.

"See how smart she is?" said Noah, scratching her ears. "I'm teaching her to sneeze. She's done it a couple of times, but she's bad about fetching. When I throw her a ball, she runs away and buries it."

Bailey laughed. She had never owned a dog—always cats. Amber had gotten a puppy, a mutt, just before Bailey moved away. Bailey liked Clover's silliness almost as much as she enjoyed watching Shadow and Sallie play together.

"Hey, look at this," said Noah as he picked up one of the old papers that Sugar had brought over and examined it more closely. "Some guy named Rudd got arrested and is in jail."

Fred said, "Let me see."

Bailey's chest felt tight. Now the twins would know about Justin's dad.

Noah asked her, "Is that Justin's father?"

Bailey nodded.

"Geez," he said. "I'd better show Mom and Dad."

Fred said, "Hey, Justin wasn't in trouble, it was his dad."

Noah said, "Doesn't matter. Look what kind of father he has. And now the sock of coins is missing from here."

"That doesn't mean anything," said Fred, giving his brother a hard look. "Be fair, Noah."

For a second Noah glared at his brother.

Bailey wondered what she should do. She didn't want Noah to not like her, but if she kept quiet, it really wouldn't be fair to Justin. If Norma Jean were here, would she care what Noah and Fred might think? No, she would defend Justin because she liked him. Norma Jean had talked with him and learned that he made things with his hands and had a pet crow. She said he had nice eyes.

Bailey finally said, "Justin's okay. Really. My sister likes him." It wasn't saying much, but she felt a little better.

Noah didn't seem to hear her. He tore the article out of the paper, folded it, and put it in his pants pocket just as Justin came in the front door.

"You're late," said Noah with a frown.

"Sorry," mumbled Justin, as he signed in.

16

Visitors for Bailey

Bailey was home washing her hands, scrubbing the dirt from under her fingernails, when Sugar's phone rang. Bailey had spent most of the afternoon at Keswick Inn, helping Miss Bekka scour the kitchen cupboards and pantry. Mr. Will and Justin made shelves for the closets in Noah and Fred's bedrooms while the twins painted an undercoat on the baseboards.

Before she had left, she heard Mr. Will tell Justin that he was a good carpenter, and that he was glad for his help. Justin actually smiled. Noah turned away and rolled his eyes.

"Bailey, the phone's for you," said her grandmother, her face crinkling.

Bailey dried her hands. *It's probably Emily,* she thought. She put the phone to her ear.

"Mom!" she shrieked. "Where are you? Really? In two days? A surprise? Wait till you see

Sallie and Shadow and everything. . . . Yeah. I love you, too. Bye." She hung up.

"Mom's coming and she has a big surprise," Bailey said.

"Did she give any hints?" asked Sugar. "Molly's surprises can be anything, you know."

"Nope, but I'm sure it will be good." Bailey gave Sugar a huge hug. "I guess she can sleep in Norma Jean's room," said Bailey, "until we leave."

Sugar suddenly looked sad and concerned. "Did she say that you would be leaving?"

"No," said Bailey, "but maybe that is the surprise."

Sugar pushed her glasses up her nose and turned to look out the window. "That would make you happy, wouldn't it?"

"I would miss you terribly," said Bailey. "I would come to visit lots of times. And we'd still have adventures." She leaned her head against her grandmother's back and hugged her tightly.

"Of course, we will," said Sugar. "Now, why don't you make sure Norma Jean's room is all fixed up for company."

As Bailey burrowed under her covers that evening, letting Shadow and Sallie pounce on her feet and hands, she worried. What if the kittens didn't like living in Florida? What would happen to all her new friends? She wouldn't be able to help with Sugar's garden and the Keswicks' house. Would Norma Jean be allowed to visit her at her mother's house? Norma Jean. She remembered how she didn't like her at all when she first met her but now wanted to see her again. And what about Sugar? Who would keep her company and help out with her projects, like her anti-littering campaign?

Bailey rolled on her side and looked out the window at the full moon. She would miss the tall trees and the sound of the rain on Sugar's roof.

Sallie curled up on Bailey's pillow and purred.

17

Missing Locket

Emily cried when Bailey said her mother was coming, and begged her not to leave.

"You're my best friend," Emily said, shoving her hair out of her face. "We're almost sisters."

"We can e-mail, and I'll come back to visit," said Bailey, feeling sadder than she had thought she would. She had hoped that Emily would be happy for her, but her friend wasn't.

In fact, Emily had been so sad all day that Bailey was relieved that she was going to the Keswicks' after school instead of to Emily's house. She thought the boys would understand why she was leaving. But the twins' reaction wasn't much better than Emily's. Noah and Fred didn't smile. They sounded cross. Justin simply said, "Figured."

Miss Bekka seemed to understand. "You will be missed, but I know you want to be with your mother. She sounds like a wonderful, adventurous person."

"I can't stay too long today," said Bailey. "I have to help Sugar fix special things to eat when Mom comes. Sugar is going to let me make a strawberry pie—one of Mom's favorites. She even got strawberries from Florida at the supermarket."

"Run along any time," said Miss Bekka. "And some day share the recipe with me."

They heard the screen door open, pushed by a small white dog with muddy paws. Clover, always overjoyed to see Bailey, raced to her, and grabbed the sponge she had been using to wash down the cabinets.

"Give me that," said Bailey, but before she could grab the dog or sponge, Clover nosed the door open and headed for her favorite digging spot under the lilac bush.

"She'll be back," said Miss Bekka. "I don't know what we're going to do when she's full grown. She'll probably be dragging the sofa or the kitchen table outside."

Bailey laughed and got another sponge out of the cleaning supplies box.

Justin came through the kitchen carrying lumber for shelves. He was wearing the tool belt that Mr. Will had given him. It was a little bit large, but Justin had punched extra holes to make it fit his waist. Mr. Will had also given him tools to use while they did their work. Bailey thought that the hammer and screwdrivers looked very shiny, like Justin had polished them.

Clover pushed her way back into the house and sped into the living room.

"Hey!" yelled Fred.

"You goofy beast," said Noah as Clover poked her black button nose in the can of white primer. Noah wiped her clean and said, "Now, shoo! Go bother someone else," but it didn't sound like he meant it.

Bailey, listening from the kitchen, realized that she would really miss the Keswicks and Clover. The dog probably wouldn't remember her by the time she came back for a visit.

She could hear Mr. Will and the twins laughing upstairs. Clover was probably playing ball with them.

Justin came back down, signed out, and said to Miss Bekka that he had to leave early today. "I'll be able to help out more tomorrow." He hung his tool belt on a peg in the back hall and left quickly.

Just before Bailey wrote down her hours, Noah stormed into the kitchen. "Mom," he said, angrily, "the silver locket is missing from the table in the sorting room."

"Who would have taken it?" asked Miss Bekka with a worried expression. "It must be under something. I'll come up and look in a minute."

Bailey heard Noah say quietly to Fred, "I'm sure it's Justin. We've got to catch him in the act." Noah saw that Bailey was listening. "And you'd better help us, or all the treasures of Keswick Inn will be gone."

18

First People

While the beautiful strawberry pie with its lattice top was in the oven, Sugar said, "I've been doing more research about the Native Americans in Virginia. I thought you might want to share this with Noah and Fred." She pushed her glasses up her nose and sat down at the kitchen table. Bailey pulled her chair close to Sugar's so she could see the books and papers.

"Many people think only of Pocahontas when they think of Virginia Indians," said Sugar.

"I saw the movie," said Bailey. "Amber and I watched it three times. I liked the music."

"The movie isn't accurate," said Sugar, "but it is a nice story. Pocahontas was only about your age, not a grown woman, when she met Captain John Smith. Long before the English arrived, the Powhatan Indians lived along the coast of Virginia.

"Powhatan was her father," said Bailey.

"Right. There are several coastal tribes within, or allied with, the Powhatan Confederacy, including the Chickahominy, Eastern Chickahominy, Mattaponi, Upper Mattaponi, Pamunkey, and the Rappahannock," Sugar said.

"Hmm," said Bailey. "Didn't we go up Pamunkey Creek in your boat?"

"Yes. Good observation," said Sugar. "There are lots of places named for the First People. Long ago there were other tribes besides those in the Powhatan Confederacy. In fact, the Manahoac Confederacy and the Monacan tribe were west of the Fall Line. They were often at war with the Powhatan tribes."

"What's a Fall Line?" said Bailey.

"It is where the waterfalls are located on a river—a natural geological division," said Sugar. "Here it is on this map of Virginia. John Smith and other explorers wouldn't have been able to navigate past the falls so they didn't know what was beyond them."

"In Florida we had the Calusa Indians and the Caloosahatchee River, but no waterfalls," said Bailey, leaning closer to Sugar.

"The Pamunkeys are especially known for their beautiful pottery. I have one of their bowls on the top shelf of one of my bookcases. The symbols on it tell the story of taking a turkey to Richmond in accordance with the treaty of 1646 between the Pamunkeys and the king.

"The Powhatans were part of a larger language group, the Algonquians," Sugar continued, as she shuffled papers that she had printed from the Internet.

"What kind of houses did they live in?"

"It says here that the Powhatans lived in yi-hakans, which were not the tent-like teepees," said Sugar. "The yi-hakans were roundish houses made with branches and sticks. They were covered with woven mats."

"I bet Noah and Fred don't know that," said Bailey, "even though they act like they know everything just because they are homeschooled." She couldn't wait to tell them what she was learning.

"It says that both the Powhatans and Monacans were farmers," said Sugar. "The men also hunted and fished. The Monacans, who spoke a Siouan language similar to the tribes out west, had burial mounds. One has been discovered in Orange County. Archeologists and historians have found artifacts on farms and near creeks."

"Which Indians lived in Louisa County?" asked Bailey.

"The Monacans were here," said Sugar. "In fact, there are grinding stones, projectile points, and tools on display in the Louisa County Museum."

"I would like to see them," said Bailey.

Sugar said, "We can do that. By the way, I found a Web site with Powhatan vocabulary words, such as 'attemous' for dog."

"I'll tell the twins," said Bailey. "Do you think Clover will come if I call her attemous?"

"I thought you would like that," said Sugar. "There are places we can visit to learn more about the First People, such as at a powwow, and at the Museum of the American Indian in Washington, D.C."

"I've never been to a powwow," said Bailey.

Sugar said, "I read in the *Lake Anna Guardian* that there will be one soon at one of the reservations. Let's see if your friends would like to go."

"How cool would that be!" said Bailey.

19

Molly Arrives

"Mom!" Bailey shouted so loudly that she was sure the Keswicks could hear her.

Molly, with her thick dark hair, sunglasses, and straw hat, climbed out of a little green sports car with tinted windows. Bailey nearly knocked her down with a hug. Molly kissed Bailey's head and face, wrapped her arms around her, and said, "I've missed you, missed you, missed you. I can't believe how tall you've grown in just a few months. This country living must be good for you."

"I missed you, too," said Bailey.

"I missed you more," said Molly, holding Bailey's shoulders in her hands. Pink polish gleamed on her nails.

Molly took off her sunglasses. Her face crinkled like Sugar's when she smiled. She looked very happy. She was wearing a gauzy, lavender long-sleeved blouse over a lime-green shirt, black capri pants, and wedge sandals—all new since Bailey had last seen her.

"I have a ton of presents for you," said Molly, giving Bailey another big smoochy kiss. In Florida, before her mother left for Costa Rica, Bailey was sometimes embarrassed by Molly's public displays of affection, but not now. She wanted a zillion PDAs.

"Do you want to see my kittens?" asked Bailey, burying her face in Molly's chest.

"Not until I give my mother a hug," said Molly, "and introduce you to my surprise." She reached around Bailey to pat Sugar on the shoulder. Bailey had forgotten about the surprise. She let go of her mother when she heard a car door open. She looked beyond Molly and saw a man get out of the passenger's side.

"Mom, Bailey, I want you to meet my Andrew. Dr. Andrew Snorge-Swinson."

Andrew. The bug guy? What's he doing here? Bailey's mouth dropped open so wide that a butterfly could have flown in.

Before she or Sugar could think of anything to say, Molly continued. "Andrew and I are headed for New York to meet with my editor and publisher. My first article, on Americans living in Costa Rica, is almost done, and they want me to write one about Andrew. His work in the field of entomology is so amazing that it may even turn into a book."

Bailey felt like she was spinning into a deep pit. Her mother and the bug guy were a blur. She felt Sugar's arms wrap around her, holding her, rescuing her.

Molly chattered on until Sugar interrupted. "Pleased to meet you, Andrew. Let's go inside. Bailey and I made dinner, and we'll figure out sleeping arrangements later."

"Oh, we won't be staying here overnight," said Molly, much too cheerfully. "We have to get to New York by noon tomorrow. This is just a quick detour to see you and Bailey." She looked at Bailey's solemn face. "I thought you'd be happier to see me."

Bailey felt like crying, but instead she smiled her best smile. "I made you a pie. Strawberry. Your favorite," said Bailey in a tight voice that she didn't recognize as her own. She turned to the house, where Sallie and Shadow were watching from behind the porch railing.

"I'm glad it's strawberry," said Molly. "Oh, and look at that rocker. Purple. My favorite color. I'll race you to the house. Go!"

Molly and Bailey bolted for the porch steps, racing like they had always done.

"This cat is Sallie, and the gray one, Shadow, is under the chair," Bailey said, pointing out her kittens to her mother.

"How absolutely adorable," said Molly, picking up Sallie and rubbing her cheek against the little black and white face. "They must be lots of fun. We have a stray cat near the lodge. I call it Murray, but the people who work there just call it *Gato*, Spanish for cat."

As Sugar and Andrew came up the walk, Bailey heard him say, "Do you mind leaving those cats outside. I'm allergic."

Molly didn't seem to be concerned. In fact she smiled happily at him. Bailey wondered how her beautiful mother could find this man even a teeny bit interesting. He had a long brown ponytail, thick round rimless glasses, bushy eyebrows, and pale-blue, watery eyes. *He looks just like a bug,* thought Bailey.

Sugar sighed, and said, "Bailey's kittens are used to being inside, but we can keep them away from you during dinner if it's a problem."

"Thanks," said Dr. Andrew Snorge-Swinson, blowing his nose into a large linen handkerchief.

"Isn't he just wonderful," Molly whispered to Bailey. "I've never met anyone quite like him."

Neither have I, thought Bailey.

"Now, let me see your room, and your homework, and the picture Norma Jean made for you," said Molly. "And I want to hear you play the clarinet. I've missed the toot-toot toodling."

Bailey led the way up the stairs.

"I love your room, girlfriend," Molly said. "It is so bright and patriotic. And what a beautiful quilt!"

Bailey showed her the report on the Contrary Creek gold mines, part of a robin's egg that she had found in the woods, a picture of Amber with Skippy, her new puppy, and one of Norma Jean.

Molly kicked off her sandals and stretched out on the bed, patting it so that Bailey would join her, just like they always did at home in Florida.

Molly said, "I'm so glad things are going well here. You and Sugar seem very happy together. I knew you would be fine."

"Sugar's great," said Bailey. "We have lots of adventures. And there are some new people—the Keswicks—fixing up an old house in the woods."

"That's what I heard," said Molly.

There was no mention of returning to Florida, or of Bailey visiting Costa Rica. Bailey was afraid to ask. She was glad she hadn't pulled her suitcase down from the attic before her mother had arrived. Then her mom would know that she had expected to go back home with her. Bailey would have felt really stupid.

"Are you still ticklish?" asked Molly.

"Are you?" asked Bailey.

They gave each other devilish looks and tried to tickle under each other's arms.

Sugar called, "Supper's on."

"Coming, Sugar," said Molly. She rumpled Bailey's hair and said, "I can't tell you how great it is to see you. I missed you very much."

"I missed you more," said Bailey, giving her mom another hug, enjoying the scent of her mother's hair, before they headed to the kitchen.

The bug man helped Sugar put the meat loaf and mashed potatoes on the table.

"I'm so glad you two have had a chance to visit," said Molly.

"His work *is* amazing," said Sugar. "Let's say grace and eat."

Bailey didn't like the way her mother smiled at Dr. Andrew Snorge-Swinson and how he looked at her with those watery eyes. He seemed to adore her. The bug man sneezed and blew his nose loudly all through dinner.

While Sugar cut the pie, Molly showed Bailey the box filled with her thick manuscript and computer disks. "Look how much I have written, but there is so much more to do. I have met so many interesting people."

She tasted the pie. "Yummy. The best. If Andrew and I decide to have a special event some day," said Molly, giving him the smile of smiles, "maybe you could make one of these for us."

Bailey and Sugar looked at each other in astonishment. *Mom has lost her mind*, thought Bailey.

In a voice that showed she meant it, Sugar said, "Bailey, sit and visit with Dr. Snorge-Swinson while your mother and I take a walk."

Molly blew a kiss as she and Sugar headed out the back door.

20

Bailey and the Bug Man

Dr. Andrew Snorge-Swinson wiped his puddling eyes and took a long sip of decaf with low-fat milk whitening it. Bailey thought he looked uncomfortable being left in the kitchen with her. She wasn't happy about it, either. He folded his handkerchief and put it back in the pocket of his denim shirt, then adjusted his glasses on his nose. Then he removed his glasses and wiped them on his shirt. He studied his fingers and looked at his thick wristwatch with four dials.

Bailey was annoyed that she had been told so firmly to stay with bug man when she wanted to hear what her mother and Sugar were talking about as they walked. But she knew she had to be on her best behavior. She forced a big smile and pushed her hair behind her ears.

"So," she said, resting her elbows on the table, "you like bugs?"

Dr. Snorge-Swinson brightened. "I'm a scientist—an entomologist. I study them. Costa Rica has some of the most interesting specimens in the world."

"Hmm," said Bailey. "What's your favorite?"

Bug man cleared his throat and said, "Actually the leafcutter ants. Of the more than 35,000 species of insects recorded in Costa Rica, I must say I'm particularly fascinated by the leafcutters. The pieces of leaves they cut and carry away eventually decay into a mulch, which the ants take care of. They grow a fungus in it that they eat. Other creatures eat the ants. You can see how important the relationship of everything is in the forest. And you? You sound like you are also interested in entomology—the study of insects."

Suddenly Bailey felt deliciously wicked. She grinned and said brightly, "I hate bugs. Hate them."

Dr. Snorge-Swinson paled and tapped his fingers nervously. "I find that hard to believe. Your mother says you are good in science."

"It's true," said Bailey. "But ants? Squoosh! Spiders? Squoosh!"

Bug man cringed.

"I'm surprised my mom didn't tell you," said Bailey.

"Tell me what?" He reached for his handkerchief and blew his nose again.

"I learned to hate them from Mom. She would make me deal with the bugs she found in Florida," said Bailey, really enjoying his discomfort. "She screamed a lot."

Dr. Snorge-Swinson sneezed again. "That's the wonderful thing about your mother," he said. "When she becomes interested in something, she changes her mind. She finds the study of entomology quite fascinating now." He cleared his throat, as if his mouth was full of crackers.

"Yeah, but what if she finds a spider in the shower?" said Bailey.

"I think she would want to learn more about it," said bug man, trying to sound positive.

Bailey realized that he might be right. There was a lot she didn't know about her mother now, but she wasn't willing to give up.

"I bet she'd whack it after she looked," Bailey said. "That's what Mom always made me do—after she screamed." She smiled sweetly at him.

Bug man wiped his nose and said, "Let's wash the dishes."

21

Gone Again

The dishes were done by the time Molly and Sugar returned. They put their arms around each other and Sugar stroked Molly's thick hair before they came back into the kitchen.

"I almost forgot your presents, Bailey," said her mom, directing Andrew to get the shopping bag full of packages from the trunk.

Bailey unwrapped a pair of leather sandals for hiking, a woven backpack, two T-shirts, one with a picture of Volcano Arenal and one with butterflies, a pan flute made of bamboo, and a scrapbook. Molly said the cover was made from banana leaves. There was also a spider pin that Molly said was a gift from Andrew, but Bailey wasn't sure if that were true. Her mother had probably bought it for him to give to her.

And there were presents for Sugar, including books about the rain forests, a bright-red dress from Panama with toucan molas on it, and three bags of Costa Rican coffee that Molly insisted were the best in the whole world.

Then, after more hugs and kisses, Molly got into the car with Dr. Andrew Snorge-Swinson.

Sugar and Bailey sat in their rockers on the porch watching the car leave the driveway.

"Do you want to talk?" Sugar finally asked, as her rocking chair creaked on the wooden porch floor.

"'Bout what?"

"'Bout your mom."

"And the bug guy?"

Sugar laughed. "Yes, and about the bug guy. I know you hoped that she was coming to take you home with her."

Bailey felt like crying. "Well, she didn't, did she? I don't care."

"I would care," said her grandmother, "and I do care, because I suspect you feel hurt right now. I feel hurt for you, and a little for me."

Bailey didn't answer. She twisted her hair.

"It's okay to cry," said Sugar, pushing her glasses up on her nose.

Bailey just rocked. She had a knot in her chest. *What am I going to tell Emily and the twins?* she wondered.

"I love you no matter what," said Sugar.

"I love you, too!" said Bailey. "Look," she said softly, pointing toward the woods.

A doe and a fawn were standing in the shadows.

"Beautiful," said Sugar, quietly. "I hope we see more of them this summer. The deer have a trail here. I usually see them at twilight or first thing in the morning."

The deer took a few more steps into the yard, flicking their white tails and turning their large ears. Then, as silently as they had arrived, they slipped back into the forest together.

Bailey sighed. *The fawn is lucky,* she thought.

22

Hayseed Muckle

"This is definitely the day for an adventure," said Sugar, as she poked her head into Bailey's bedroom. Molly's presents were still heaped on a chair.

"You've been so busy working at the Keswicks, I think it's a good time to take a break and go boating—maybe fishing," said Sugar.

Bailey wiped the sleep from her eyes.

"Would you like to invite anyone?"

Bailey shook her head. Normally she would have called Emily, but Emily was sleeping over at Beth's house, and she knew Noah and Fred would be busy working at their place because it was the weekend.

It didn't take them long to get ready. Bailey made her PB&J sandwiches, which Sugar said were the best in the world, while her grandmother hitched the little boat trailer to the pickup. Sugar placed the fishing poles and a red gas can in the back of the truck.

There wasn't a cloud in the sky and only a slight breeze.

"We'll stop for gas and bait on the way," Sugar said, turning the ignition.

Bailey liked the little stores around the lake that sold gas, fried chicken, barbecue sandwiches, delicious biscuits, and eggs—anything you'd need for a picnic—and fishing supplies. The stores were always crowded with people who visited the lake on vacation, as well as the year-rounders.

As Sugar put oil in the gas can and then filled the can with gas, Bailey saw a large man wearing navy-blue coveralls, a dark red shirt, and straw hat walking over. He called out, "Well, Miss Sugar, how y'all doing?"

"Hayseed, good to see you!"

Bailey got out of the truck so she could hear their conversation. Sometimes her grandmother became so involved talking with people she lost track of time, especially if they were discussing her favorite topics of water pollution, littering, or saving trees.

Bailey leaned up against the truck, just like Sugar and Hayseed were doing. Sure enough, they were talking about trees.

"No, I don't understand it, either," said Sugar. "Why do people buy property filled with trees and then bulldoze them? *All* of them."

"There ought to be a law," said Hayseed, as he rolled a piece of hay in his mouth. Bailey watched in fascination as the yellow stem vanished, then popped out between his lips while he talked.

"The worst of it is that some builders buy land, clear it, and put up a house before they even have a buyer. The buyer never knows how beautiful the lot used to be with lovely shade trees," he said.

"And the trees are good for birds and oxygen," interrupted Bailey.

"This must be Miss Bailey," said Hayseed slowly, the hay reappearing.

"My wonderful granddaughter, and one of the wild women of the family," said Sugar. "She's adventurous, just like me."

"I don't mean to hold you up," said Hayseed. The piece of hay was gone again. Bailey worried that he might have swallowed it, but it soon reappeared.

"Heard a large piece of property in your neighborhood may be going on the market. Hope you folks don't lose a lot of trees along your road if it does," he said.

Sugar looked concerned. "Thanks. I'll see what I can find out."

"I'm about to call Will Keswick. I heard he needs a handyman," said Hayseed.

"Good," said Sugar. "He needs more help than just the kids, although they've been working hard."

"Hayseed's a funny name," said Bailey when they were on the road to the boat ramp.

"That isn't his real name, of course," said Sugar, with her crinkly smile. "His real name is H. Z. Muckle. Because he would never tell anyone what the initials stood for, he got a nickname—Hayseed. He's a good friend, and a member of my environmental group."

The little metal boat, the color of an army uniform, slid easily off the trailer. Bailey stood on the dock and held the lines while Sugar parked the trailer, then returned with the life jackets and gas can.

"Almost forgot the poles and bait," she said, nodding to Bailey to go get them.

The engine started right up. Bailey pushed the boat away from the wooden dock.

"One thing that makes the waterfront so beautiful is all the trees," said Sugar. "I'm glad that so many people kept them when they built their houses at Lake Anna."

Sugar steered them to her favorite fishing hole near the third dike. "I always catch something here," she said. "Well, almost always."

She showed Bailey how to bait the hook with a wiggly worm—a night crawler.

"Yuck," said Bailey. She didn't like the way it felt or putting the hook through it.

"It's like dessert for fish," said Sugar.

Bailey held her pole over the side, dangling the line into the dark water, and watched the night crawler disappear. Sugar put a red-and-white bobber on her line and cast it out away from the boat. The bobber floated on the surface while the worm drifted below, carried down by a small gray weight tied on the line.

"Yikes!" said Bailey. She felt a tug.

"Yank it fast," said Sugar, "to set the hook."

Bailey wasn't fast enough and the hook came up wormless. She wanted to ask Sugar to bait her hook again, but knew her grandmother would say she was busy fishing so that Bailey would learn to do it herself. That was icky part of being a wild woman.

Bailey took a deep breath, stuck her hand in the cardboard container of worms, pulled one out, and looped the hook through it just as Sugar had demonstrated. She could see her grandmother looking at her out of the corner of her eye as Sugar reeled in her bobber, and cast again.

"Be lucky, yucky worm," Bailey whispered, as she let her hook down in the dark lake.

She had never gone fishing in Florida. Sometimes her mom talked about it, but when Saturdays came, they usually decided to go to the beach instead. The bug man didn't look like he did anything but stick his eyes up against a microscope or crawl around in the jungle looking for creepy things, so her mom probably wasn't fishing in Costa Rica, either.

There was another yank on her line. This time Bailey tugged back fast. It felt like the pole was going to fly out of her hands.

"Sugar, a fish! A big fish!"

"Reel it in slowly. It will fight, and double back, and maybe even jump out of the water, but just be steady. I'll get the net."

As Sugar started to reel in her own line so that she could help Bailey, she also felt a tug.

"I've got one, too," Sugar said. "I told you this was a good fishing spot."

Bailey thought her arms would break as the fish pulled and pulled. Occasionally she could see something about a foot long splashing in the water, but then it would dive again.

"Fiddlesticks," said Sugar, as her fish got away. She reached for the net and put it in the water by the side of the boat. "See if you can steer your fish into it. There, we've got it." Sugar held up the dripping net. "It's a striper, a beauty. What should we do with it?"

"Let's let it go," said Bailey.

"Good idea."

Sugar carefully removed Bailey's hook and placed the striper back in the water.

"Bye, fish," said Bailey. The knot she had felt since her mother had come and gone vanished as the striped bass swam away.

"I've got an idea," said Sugar. "I didn't really want to clean and cook fish for dinner, so let's go out—it's not half-price hamburger night, but a burger sounds mighty good."

"Deal," said Bailey, as she took a deep breath and picked out another worm.

23

Another Discovery

"No way!" said Fred, as Bailey described catching the big fish. "Dad said he'd take us fishing sometime, but he is always so busy with this house."

Noah said, "I caught a fish once when I was little. It was in a duck pond. I thought the ducks were going to peck me with their bills. They came up on the grass and quacked at me." He flashed a big grin.

Bailey was relieved that neither boy asked about her mom's visit. They would be leaving for home later in the afternoon. Noah wasn't sure when they would return.

Mr. Will called from upstairs, "Hey, come on up. I want you to see the shelves. Justin and I are making progress with the bedrooms."

Clover raced up the stairs as if she was the one who had been called. Her fur was getting longer and fluffier, and her paws were always dirty from digging.

"If only she'd put the dirt back when she's done with a hole," said Miss Bekka, "but it always vanishes. Our lawn has more holes than a donut factory."

But Miss Bekka didn't seem terribly upset about Clover. The white dog made everyone laugh, even when they were tired at the end of the day.

The boys admitted that the shelves Justin made were excellent. Fred said there was room for his model race cars and soccer trophies. Even Noah seemed impressed by how smooth the boards were.

"My helper, here," said Mr. Will, "is an excellent craftsman. He measures carefully—twice—before he cuts a board. He makes sure everything is level. He has more patience than I do."

Justin smiled as he looked at his feet.

"He's going to put up bookshelves after the walls are painted. First we're going to fix the closets in the guest rooms and repair cabinets in the guest baths. And look what we found in this closet," said Mr. Will.

Noah, Fred, and Bailey gathered around. Mr. Will pulled an antique silver watch out of a velvety sack. "It was down in the corner behind a box of old leather shoes," he said.

"Wow!" said Noah. "Another treasure."

"Put it in the sorting room," said his father. He handed the watch to Bailey, who returned it to the sack. Noah followed her.

"Did you see how Justin was looking at that watch?" he said. "I'll bet he wants to steal it, too."

Bailey didn't know what to say. Noah seemed so certain about Justin. Why did she feel she should defend him?

"I don't think he's like that," she finally said, as she put the little bag on the table. She sat in a chair and looked at some of the other treasures—a leather-bound book of rhymes, a cloth doll with button eyes, a magazine from 1906 with beauty tips, and wire-rim spectacles with glass so dark that you couldn't see through them. Mr. Will thought they might have been used to look at something really bright, like an eclipse of the sun.

"But you don't really know him, do you, dude?" said Noah, with a frown on his usually cheerful face. "I'm thinking about setting a trap to catch the thief. Too many good things we found here are missing lately. Somebody's taking them and I want to know who. Will you help?"

How could Bailey say no to her new friend with his comical, yellow sticking-out hair.

"Okay," she said.

"Good," said Noah. "Fred's in. Instead of being the twins, we'll be the triplets. The detective triplets." His green eyes were laughing again.

24

The Triplets

Justin looked at his watch and hurriedly left, as he had every day that week. Noah checked the sorting table, but found nothing was missing.

"He probably knows we're watching him," said Noah to Bailey and Fred, who were putting tools away and picking up the newspapers that had been used while they painted.

"When we come back next time, we'll figure out how to catch him in the act. Then we can go to Dad with proof, and that will be the end of Mr. Justin Rudd."

With that, Noah held out his right hand. Bailey and Fred put theirs out and they shook them together. "Triplets forever," said Noah, looking pleased.

"Triplets forever," said Bailey and Fred.

Bailey looked at Fred. He didn't look happy about setting a trap for Justin, but as Noah said, somebody *was* stealing things from the sorting room. Noah was just protecting family property. Bailey knew if someone were stealing things from Sugar's house, she would probably do the same.

"I bet Sugar has detective books," said Bailey. "She has a lot of books in her library. I'll look up plans for a trap."

Bailey glanced out the window and saw a shiny blue pickup pull in the driveway and stop next to the van in which Miss Bekka was placing suitcases and coolers. The man looked familiar. Bailey realized that it was Hayseed. She wondered if he had another piece of hay in his mouth.

Mr. Will walked over from the barn and shook Hayseed's hand. They talked briefly and he handed Hayseed a set of keys, then Hayseed left.

"Who was that?" Fred asked his father as the triplets went outside.

"Hayseed Muckle," interrupted Bailey. "He's a friend of Sugar's."

"Hayseed is going to help us with the house," said Mr. Will. "He's an excellent handyman. He and his crew will work on things while we are gone. I think with his help we will be able to move in and open Keswick Inn much sooner than we had expected."

"Ready to go?" asked Miss Bekka, looking at her watch. "We've got a long drive ahead, and you boys need to get caught up on your schoolwork or your teacher will get after you." She smiled as she pointed a finger at herself.

"See ya," yelled Fred.

Noah shouted, "Bye, dude," as Bailey waved. She watched her friends leave, then ran down the path through the woods to Sugar's house.

25

More E-mails

While Sugar fixed spaghetti with Bailey's favorite meatballs, Bailey checked e-mail. She had been so busy that she hadn't looked at it for a while.

There were two from Amber and one from Norma Jean—the first she had received since her half sister and their dad had returned to Guam. She opened it:

From:<pjfish2005@yermail.net>
To: "Bailey"<baileyfish@gmail.com>
Sent: 3:05 p.m.
Subject: Hi

Sis: I miss you, Sugar and the kittens. The plane ride was bumpy but we got home OK. I told everyone about you. I want Dad to find a job in Virginia near you. Tell Justin I keep my best pencils in the box he gave me. How are Emily and Amber? SCR, Norma Jean.

Bailey replied:

From: "Bailey"<baileyfish@gmail.com>
To: <pjfish2005@yermail.net>
Sent: 5:36 p.m.
Subject: *reply*

Noah, Fred, Justin and I are helping fix up the old house. Emily wants to help when school is out, but she's been busy. We get paid. I caught a big fish when Sugar and I went boating. We didn't keep it. Sallie naps on your bed sometimes. Sugar said we can go to a powwow soon. Got to go. SCR Bailey

Amber's first, from the day before said:

From: jbs25@yourmail.net
To: "Bailey"<baileyfish@gmail.com>
Sent: 6:14 p.m.
Subject: Hey

I'm sick of school. All we do is get ready for tests. SCR Amber

The second, from today, read:

From: jbs25@yourmail.net
To: "Bailey"<baileyfish@gmail.com>
Sent: 5:02 p.m.
Subject: Answer me

Bailey, where are you? Why haven't you answered me? SCR Amber

Bailey wrote:

From: "Bailey"<baileyfish@gmail.com>
To: jbs25@yermail.net
Sent: 5:57 p.m.
Subject: Sorry

I've been really busy. We've got to solve a mystery at Keswick Inn. Things keep disappearing. Do you know how to catch a thief? SCR
Bailey

Bailey sighed.

26

The Piano

Martha Keswick and Sugar tried to arrange for the piano to be delivered while Bailey was at school so that she would be surprised, but the movers were late. Their small van was backed up to the front porch just as the school bus dropped Bailey off at the end of the driveway.

Bailey ran to the house so she could watch. One of the men lifted the roll-up door of the van. The piano was covered with blue quilted blankets. The three men placed a ramp from the truck's tailgate to the porch and slowly wheeled the piano on it.

"Be careful," fretted Martha Keswick. "It is old and special, like me."

"Don't worry, ma'am," said one of the movers. "We move antiques and big things all the time."

They lifted the piano over the threshold, and slowly pushed it down the front hall to Sugar's library. Bailey was afraid to look. What if it didn't fit through the library door? The movers tipped it on one end, which made Martha Keswick even more nervous.

"Oh, please be careful. It was my mother's."

"Yes, ma'am," grunted another mover. "No scratches."

Bailey looked out the front door. She didn't want to watch them drop it. Martha Keswick's worries made her worry, too.

"Okay, Francisco," said the third man. "Easy does it."

Bailey turned around. The movers and piano had disappeared into the library. One man came back down the hall carrying the blue quilted blankets.

"All done," he said to Bailey. "Not a ding."

Bailey could hear the sound of jazz coming from the library. She peeked in. Francisco was playing a tune—it sounded like his funny version of "Take Me Out to the Ball Game." He took a bow as they all clapped. As he collected his check from Sugar, Bailey heard a different sort of music.

"Get down," she scolded. Shadow was walking on the keys.

"Needs tuning," said Mrs. Keswick, "but there was no point in doing that before she was moved."

Bailey sat on the piano bench and put her hands on the yellowed ivory keys. Amber had shown her how to play "Chopsticks," but that was all she knew. She tried a few notes.

"It has a lovely tone," said Sugar. "Next, we need to find a teacher for both of us."

"Hayseed's wife, Peg, accompanies her church choir. I think she gave lessons years ago," said Martha Keswick. "Maybe she could be talked into teaching again."

"Great idea," said Sugar.

Bailey lifted the lid of the piano bench seat. "Look, here are a bunch of piano books."

"Looks like we are ready to start," said Sugar.

27

Property for Sale

Bailey was waiting for the school bus when Sugar returned from her morning walk. She carried two plastic bags of trash that she had picked up along the road.

"Hayseed was right," Sugar said. "There is a new FOR SALE sign across the road and down a piece. I've got to find out what's going on."

Bailey saw that her grandmother was concerned. She gave her a hug as the yellow bus pulled up. Emily wasn't in her usual seat. Bailey remembered her friend had left a message on Sugar's answering machine, but Bailey had been so busy finishing her homework the night before that she had forgotten to call her back. *I wonder if she's sick?*

The bus stopped to pick up Justin. Bailey remembered she had a message for him from her half sister.

"Norma Jean says hi," she said. "She likes the crow box."

Justin seemed pleased. "Tell her that Chuck is flying a little better." He walked to the back of the bus and took his seat with two rowdy friends. They teased Justin about talking with Florida girl until he told them to knock it off, like he meant it.

As Bailey looked at the rolling fields and woods, she thought about the afternoon that she, Sugar, and Norma Jean had gone to see the Rudds. Justin let them feed corn to Chuck, a crow with a damaged wing that he had rescued when it was a baby.

How could Justin be the thief? she wondered. *He doesn't talk much, but he takes care of his mother and little sisters. I don't know why Noah is so against him.* Bailey rested her chin on her hand as she pressed her nose against the window.

When the bus returned in the afternoon, Bailey got a good look at the FOR SALE sign. She couldn't read all the words on it, but she realized the sign *was* very close to Sugar's land. *No wonder Sugar is worried*, she thought.

28

Sugar Calls a Meeting

There was another message from Emily on the answering machine. Bailey could barely understand what her friend said, so she called her immediately.

Emily had a sore throat and was losing her voice. Bailey felt terrible that she hadn't phoned her back the day before. And she felt guilty that she was spending so much time with Noah and Fred, instead of with Emily.

"Mom says I can help the Keswicks when I feel better," Emily whispered hoarsely.

Bailey told her there was plenty to do at the old house and gave her the homework assignments.

"Maybe you could go boating with us when you feel better," said Bailey.

"Okay," said Emily, coughing. "I gotta lie down again."

As Bailey spread her homework out on the kitchen table, she heard Sugar phone Hayseed.

"Sure," said Sugar. "I'm willing to meet with them. Let's see what we can work out. Good idea."

"What's up?" asked Bailey when her grandmother hung up the phone.

"Hayseed found out that the people who want to buy the land across the road need the neighbors' approval to develop it the way they want. This gives us a chance to talk them into saving as many trees as possible," said Sugar. "It's worth a try. We're inviting them to meet with us."

"Can I go to the meeting?" asked Bailey.

"Sure," said Sugar.

Bailey did her math first, and then her history homework as Sugar called other neighbors to tell them about the meeting.

Bailey needed to spend time getting ready for the end-of-the-year tests coming up soon. She didn't want to wait until the weekend to do the extra studying in case the Keswicks came back again. It was too much fun helping them out.

The phone rang. "For you," said Sugar, handing it to her.

"Mom?" Bailey was surprised to hear her mother's voice. For a moment she wondered if her mother was calling to say she was coming to visit again, or had changed her mind and would be taking Bailey to Costa Rica.

"We're flying back to San José tomorrow," said her mom. "I wanted to say good-bye before we get back to the jungle where telephoning is difficult. And I thought you would want to know that the publisher *does* want me to do a book about Andrew."

Bailey was silent.

"Bailey? Are you there? This is really huge," said her mom. "Once it's done, we'll be on book tours, and television—who knows what else. He's a very important man in his field. Hey, aren't you happy for me?"

"Yeah, that's awesome, Mom," said Bailey, finally. She tried to sound cheerful, but she wasn't.

"I love you very much," said Molly. "You'll get the first autographed copy."

"Love you, too," said Bailey, handing the phone back to Sugar.

Bailey walked over to the window and looked out. She put her hands in her pockets. Three chickadees and a grosbeak were sorting through seeds at the bird feeder.

A book about the bug man. Give me a break, thought Bailey. Now she knew one thing for certain: Her mother wasn't going to be coming home soon.

She felt Sugar's arms encircling her as her grandmother said, "Let's go refill the feeder."

29

Hard to Sleep

Before turning off her light at nine o'clock, Bailey read more of *The Secret Garden,* then looked at the pictures of her mother, father, and baby Bailey in the little photo album that Sugar had given her. She couldn't sleep.

Bailey counted the deep, slow bongs from the grandfather's clock as she looked out her dormer window at the bright stars. Ten.

Shadow and Sallie were curled around her head, leaving little room for her to roll over if she had wanted to. But she didn't. Not yet.

Instead of relaxing with her sleeping cats, Bailey was wide awake as if it were a sunny spring morning full of crisp air and adventure.

Bailey heard Sugar's classical music on her CD player. The music was as soft and tender as her grandmother's sweater, the blue one with a zipper and two big pockets.

When she thought about her mom, she felt empty—like her mother had ripped open a Christmas present and thrown away both the pretty paper and the gift. Bailey wondered if her mother would stop being interested in bug man if she went to visit her in Costa Rica. Maybe her mother would be surprised that Bailey had saved money for the airplane ride, and she would realize how much Bailey missed her.

Molly would tell bug man that she wasn't going to finish writing about him and that she and Bailey would go back to Florida after she showed Bailey the rain forest and the volcano.

Bailey decided that she should tell Sugar about her trip plans. She put on her scuffy slippers and padded down the steps. Her kittens didn't stir.

The flute music made her think of waves on a beach as she neared the library where Sugar often read before going to bed.

From the doorway Bailey could see her grandmother stretched out in her green recliner; her glasses had slipped down her nose and her new book about the Powhatans was in her lap. Sugar was snoring.

Bailey was torn between laughing at the deep, oinking snores and crying because she had hoped to find Sugar awake so she could get one of her grandmother's special hugs.

She waited for a moment, watching her grandmother breathe so deeply that it looked like the book would crash to the floor. Bailey carefully removed the book, inserted the bookmark—a torn piece of magazine cover—and put it on a side table. Then she covered Sugar with a woven, blue-striped Mexican blanket that was folded on the back of the couch.

When Bailey climbed back into bed, Shadow and Sallie were still on the pillow. Bailey wrapped her arms around her large bear, her best one, and took one last look at the night sky before she closed her eyes. *I wonder if the moon and stars look the same in Costa Rica.*

30

Meeting with Hadley Hudson

Sugar picked up Bailey after school on Thursday so that she could attend the meeting with the man who wanted to buy the land. The meeting was in the back room of a restaurant where there was space for all the neighbors to have seats. A waitress wearing a pink T-shirt with a gorilla pictured on it was taking orders. Bailey and Sugar asked for water with lemon as they sat down. Their metal chairs with red seats scraped loudly as they pulled them closer to the table.

Bailey looked around the room. There were several people she knew coming in. Hayseed, Emily and her parents, Mr. and Mrs. Dover, Martha Keswick, plus Henry and Alice Smith.

"Sit here," Bailey mouthed, patting the chair next to hers. Emily quickly sat down. Her face was pale, except for a red nose. She had missed school all week and was coughing, but her voice was returning.

"I didn't know you were coming," said Bailey.

"Mom said I needed to get out," said Emily, dragging her chair closer to Bailey's. "I don't feel great, but the doctor gave me new stuff for my cough."

The land buyer's representative rushed in with a briefcase and large rolls of papers. He wore a tight gray suit and yellow tie with black diamonds on it. His pudgy face was flushed and sweaty, like he had been running.

Sugar and Hayseed stood up to welcome him.

"Sorry I'm late," said the man. "I'm Hadley Hudson, the developer's agent. Just call me Bruno," he said to them.

Sugar suggested that Hadley Hudson— Bruno—tape his large maps to an easel so that everyone could see them. The waitress brought him a pitcher of sweet tea and a large glass of ice.

"What's this about?" whispered Emily, unwrapping a cherry cough drop, then popping it in her mouth.

"Sugar's trying to get them to save trees on our road instead of knocking them all down to build a bunch of houses and stores," said Bailey.

"Good," whispered Emily. "I like trees."

A few more people came in and took seats. The room was filling up with Sugar's friends and neighbors. Bruno seemed surprised that the crowd was so large. He wiped his forehead

with his handkerchief and introduced himself to the group. He pointed to his map that showed the county roads, then pointed out how the development would be created. He said there would probably be 280 homes and a small shopping center with a restaurant and boutique shops.

Bailey looked at Sugar's face. Her grandmother appeared thoughtful, but not upset at the housing plan. Sugar rubbed her chin and ran her fingers through her short, dyed-brown hair.

"Bruno," she said, after taking a closer look at the map, "it would appear that you need to have the zoning changed if you want to build the shopping center. Right?"

Bruno nervously wiped his brow again, and straightened his tie. "That's right, Miss Sugar."

"That zoning change needs community support. Right?"

"That would certainly help," Bruno said. Bailey thought he looked nervous. There was murmuring in the room.

"I think the community will support you if you can give us some guarantees in writing," Sugar said with a pleasant smile.

"What sort of guarantees?" Bruno asked.

"That we can work together on a plan to save trees, as a buffer along the road and within the development. We know many trees will need to be cut, but we don't want to see bulldozers just knocking down everything," said Sugar.

Bailey heard the other adults saying loudly, "That's right." "You bet." "Save the trees." "No more clear-cutting."

Bruno looked around the room in surprise. "I think we can work this out without too much trouble," he said. "I'll get back to you as soon as I get some answers."

"Good," said Sugar. "Let us know. Like I said, it looks like you have a very nice project planned. We just want to make sure that the beautiful trees are saved. If they are, they will make your development even more attractive." She reached out her hand and he shook it.

Everyone applauded except Emily, who was unwrapping a new packet of tissues.

As the room emptied, Bailey said, "Emily, can you come over soon? You can help Noah and Fred catch someone who is stealing stuff from Keswick Inn."

"Cool," said Emily. "I like mysteries."

Sugar said it was too soon to celebrate that the trees would be saved. There was a lot that could go wrong, but she was pleased so far.

"I think we got his attention," she said. "He knows that there is a large group of people who care and will fight for the trees."

"I was proud of you," said Bailey as they got in Sugar's truck. Sugar reached over and patted her hand.

"It's part of being a wild woman," said her grandmother. "We need to help the wildest woman of them all—Mother Earth."

Bailey couldn't wait to e-mail Norma Jean.

31

E-mail Surprises

While Sugar fixed a chicken-noodle casserole for supper, Bailey turned on the computer. Her heart pounded when she saw there was an e-mail from her father—the first he had sent her since he had gone back to Guam.

From: <pjfish2005@yermail.net>
To: "Bailey"<baileyfish@gmail.com>
Sent: 6:50 p.m.
Subject: hello

Hi Bailey--I'll bet you are surprised to hear from your dad. Flora and the boys are looking forward to meeting you when we move to the States. I don't know how soon, but I'm working on it. Norma Jean is already packing. :) You and I have a lot of catching up to do. Love, Dad

Then it really was true that the family might be moving closer. Bailey was both excited and worried. She wondered if her half brothers and her stepmother were nice. She was still a little nervous about her dad, and whether he would try to take her away from Sugar or her mom.

Bailey wasn't sure what to say to him, so she read an e-mail from Norma Jean.

From: <pjfish2005@yermail.net>
To: "Bailey"<baileyfish@gmail.com>
Sent: 7:15 p.m.
Subject: hi
Sis, I can't wait to come back and help out at the old house. My mom says it's OK for me to work there, but Paulie and Sam are too little. We went on a speedboat. It was so fast my hair went straight back behind me. I drew a picture and I'll send it to you. How are the kittens? SCR, Norma Jean

Bailey quickly replied:

From: "Bailey"<baileyfish@gmail.com>
To: <pjfish2005@yermail.net>
Sent: 7:25 p.m.
Subject: work

There is a lot of work to do. Mr. Will wants to move in sooner than they planned, so he is hiring more grown-ups to do the big jobs. Tomorrow I'm going to go through boxes of old books and letters we found in one of the sheds. They kinda stink and have bugs, but Miss Bekka said some might be valuable. SCR Bailey

"Bailey, I need help setting the table," called Sugar. "Supper is almost ready and I fixed something special—homemade biscuits and a big tossed salad."

As Bailey put the silverware on the yellow woven place mats, she said, "Guess what? I got an e-mail from my father."

"Really!" said Sugar as she took the chicken-noodle casserole from the oven. "How did you feel about that?"

"Okay, I guess," said Bailey. "You can read it. He says they are going to move back here somewhere."

"I suspected that they might," said Sugar, washing her hands in the sink.

"I don't want to go to live with them," said Bailey. "I want to stay with you . . . or Mom."

"Not to worry," said Sugar. "Remember, I am your guardian while your mother travels."

"I know," said Bailey. She folded paper napkins and put them under the forks. Then she took the salt and pepper shakers, which were shaped like tomatoes, off the counter and put them on the table.

"I really think everything is going to be okay," said Sugar. "Your dad told me he wants to get to know you after all these years."

"I haven't e-mailed him back yet," said Bailey.

"You probably have a lot to tell him," said Sugar, patting her on the shoulder.

"Maybe after supper," said Bailey.

32

One Mystery Solved

Miss Bekka, Noah, and Fred were unpacking the boxes in the sorting room when Bailey arrived.

"Sorry I'm late," she said, "but I had to feed the kittens and clean the litter box."

"We just started," said Miss Bekka. "These books and papers are very old, so handle them carefully. If something is too damaged, I'll have a look and we will probably throw it out. But we'll save what we can from the Emmett library."

Bailey opened the dusty carton and gently lifted out the first book. She blew grit off the blue hardcover book titled *Don Juan*. The inside pages had yellowed. Many had brown spots and torn edges. She briefly looked at a sketch of Lord Byron, the poet, before putting the book in a stack of what Miss Bekka called "keepers."

By the time Bailey opened the third carton, her nose itched from the dust. The third box contained envelopes with letters, papers and a photo album.

"Yuck," said Bailey, as a spider scuttled out. *Maybe I should mail it to the bug man.* She smiled to herself.

Among the loose papers, thin and yellowed, were copies of old bills and receipts for taxes, building supplies, livestock feed, a new plow, and six yards of calico fabric.

Bailey also found a map of what the countryside had looked like before the Virginia Electric and Power Company created Lake Anna to cool water for the nuclear power plant.

Then she studied the letters. Just like Sugar had kept boxes of all the letters she had ever received from Bailey's mother and other relatives, old Mr. Emmett had saved letters addressed to him.

Bailey carefully opened one dated September 21, 1912.

The handwriting, although elegant, was difficult to read.

My dearest Edgar—

The train ride back to Dayton was hot and dusty, and I am afraid the black-eyed Susans you picked for me did not last well. I plan to dry them, however, between the pages of my family Bible so that I can keep them forever. It was such a lovely visit to your beautiful farm near the Allah Cooper mine. I will think carefully about your proposal of marriage. With great affection,

Marie Morton Peterson

Bailey opened another dated October 22, 1912.

My darling Edgar—

After much thought and prayer, I have decided that I would be happy to be your wife. I know it will be a different life for me being in the country and away from the theater, but I will be fine. The lovely locket you sent by way of your friend Harrison is a perfect engagement gift. So yes, I am yours.

It was signed MMP inside a hand-drawn heart.

"Miss Bekka, Miss Bekka," said Bailey with excitement. "The locket mystery is solved, even though the silver locket is still missing. Look at this."

Miss Bekka read the letters as Bailey looked further inside the box.

She found a letter postmarked November 26 from Dayton. It was not in MMP's handwriting. She looked at the signature. It was from Harrison Weaver.

Dear friend,

I regret to inform you that there has been a terrible accident. Marie was thrown from her riding horse, Betsy, yesterday in a cornfield. Betsy evidently stumbled in a hole and Marie lived only long enough to ask that I return the locket to you with her love.

This was a sad day for all of us, and sadder for you, dear friend.

Harrison

"Wow!" said Bailey. "That explains why Mr. Emmett had the locket and why it was hidden away."

"We'll put these letters with the locket when we find it," said Miss Bekka. "Good job, Bailey."

Noah whispered to Fred, "If we find it. Ha. We know who took the locket, and the thief is going to pay."

33

Powwow

Sugar and Miss Bekka studied the directions to the reservation east of Richmond. "We should be there in an hour," said Sugar, as she buckled her seat belt in the Keswicks' van.

Fred and Noah sat in the third row of seats, while Bailey and Emily, with her huge box of tissues, sat in the middle ones.

"Too bad Will and Justin couldn't come," said Sugar.

"Too much work to do today," said Miss Bekka, putting on her sunglasses.

"Betcha don't know about powwows," said Noah, poking Bailey.

"Oww! Do too," she said. "There's dancing, drumming, and singing. People dress up in native outfits. We read about powwows in school."

"Betcha don't know about the Chickahominy Indians," said Noah, poking her again.

"If you're so smart, you tell me," said Bailey, trying to poke him back.

"They are one of the eight state-recognized tribes in Virginia—but not part of the original Powhatan Confederacy," said Noah, trying to sound like a teacher. "We decided to study them in homeschool this week." His voice had a "so there" sound to it that was mildly annoying to Bailey because she and Sugar also had been learning about the Indians.

"Chickahominy means 'coarse pound corn people,'" said Fred. "I did my homework, too. Hey, there are signs to the powwow."

"Well, Mattaponi means 'people at the landing place,'" said Bailey. "Sugar and I did our homework, too!"

"There sure are a lot of cars," said Emily, as they drove into the parking area, "and people camping in tents."

"I don't think there is much danger of you getting lost," said Miss Bekka as they entered the gate, "but please watch out for each other."

Noah headed for a booth that sold spears with feathers and ornate headdresses. Fred tagged along with him as the girls wandered

off to look at the dancers, who were assembling in the center of the powwow.

"Look at all the kids dressed up," said Emily. Her voice was coming back, but she was still hoarse.

"Those girls are called jingle dancers," said Bailey. "See all the little silver cones that bounce and jingle on their dresses? And those women with shawls are the fancy dancers. I've been reading about them."

"Cool," said Emily.

"And there is one more kind—the traditional dancers. Sugar says they walk slowly to show their respect for the earth," Bailey said.

Sugar and Miss Bekka stopped to talk with the tribal chief wearing a soft brown buckskin jacket and a beautiful headdress made with beads and feathers. Just then the dancers were called to the arena to get ready for the welcome ceremonies.

Dancers, and an honor guard of military veterans carrying flags, entered the arena—called the sacred circle—and slowly processed around it.

"Aren't those dresses beautiful?" whispered Emily, as the dancers passed them. They wore beads or feathers, and colorful garb that were not at all alike. The announcer said that many different tribes were represented that day from all around the country.

"Sugar told me that only some people, like the veterans or elders, wear eagle feathers," whispered Bailey. "And if one falls during a dance, there is a special ceremony to protect it because it represents a fallen warrior."

"Oh," said Emily. "I didn't know that." She took a tissue out of her jacket pocket and blew her nose loudly.

"Shhh," said Bailey.

They heard the emcee announce the Victory Dance—victory over all the hardships that generations of Indians had encountered.

"Remember our elders. Remember Wounded Knee. Remember the Trail of Tears. Remember Jamestown. Dancers, dance in place. Stand tall and be proud. Dance hard," the announcer said.

His words made Bailey sad, but also curious about what the dancers were remembering. *Maybe Sugar knows,* thought Bailey.

Bailey and Emily stood on tiptoes to see over people who were sitting in chairs in front of them. They silently watched the proud dancers dance in place as the singers sat in a small circle around a large drum that they beat in unison.

Bailey felt something bumping her back. She turned to face Noah, who had bought one of the toy spears topped with feathers. He grinned.

"Shhh," she said. "I want to watch the dancers."

"Just look at what Fred bought," said Noah.

Fred pointed to a leather strap around his neck. An arrowhead hung from it.

"Cool," said Emily. "I want to buy beads for Nanny and Howie. I saw them over there." She pointed to a tent near the refreshment booths.

After they watched three more dances, Bailey followed her friend to the tent with the green-and-white striped canvas top. While Emily looked at various packages of beads, Bailey admired the dreamcatchers made of string, beads and feathers. She thought one would look nice in her dormer window. The clerk, wearing a blousy green dress and a silver-and-turquoise necklace, said, "Do you know the story of the dreamcatcher?"

Bailey said, "No, ma'am."

The woman said, "Many tribes make them now, but they originated with the Ojibwe and Chippewa in Wisconsin. Parents hung them over cradles so that their babies would be protected from bad dreams and evil. See, they look like webs to catch the dreams. The originals were dyed red."

"Is the feather just for decoration?" asked Bailey.

"The feather in the center means breath or air," said the woman. "I made these myself. They aren't too hard to make."

Bailey touched the web and the spotted brown feather of one she especially liked. She fingered the five dollar bill she had in a change purse in her pocket.

She realized that if she spent her money on a dreamcatcher, she would have less saved for a plane ticket to Costa Rica. She decided not to buy it.

"Here you girls are," said Sugar coming up behind her. "I think that we will have to be heading for home after we watch one more dance."

"Okay," said Bailey, looking back longingly at the beautiful dreamcatcher.

34

Piano Lessons

"It's arranged," said Sugar, as Bailey made her lunch for school. "I spoke with Peg Muckle last night and she said she'd be delighted to teach us piano. In fact, she's coming by today."

"You can go first," said Bailey, as she sliced her tuna sandwich in half.

"You're the one with the proper hands for playing according to Miss Dolly. Remember? I'll probably be all thumbs," said Sugar.

"We'll both get gold or silver stars," said Bailey, as she put the sandwich and an apple in a brown paper sack.

Emily wasn't in school again. Justin barely looked at Bailey as he got on the bus for the ride home. She stared out the window and thought about the piano lesson.

Mrs. Muckle's maroon car was parked in Sugar's yard when Bailey hopped down the bus steps. As she neared the library she heard a woman say, "Put your thumb on middle C."

Bailey opened the door quietly and tiptoed down the hall to the library. Sugar was having her first lesson. Mrs. Muckle was showing her the notes and how to play "Lightly Row." Bailey smiled. Sugar didn't know how to read music very well, but Bailey did from playing the clarinet. Bailey could tell by how her grandmother looked back and forth from her hands to the music that she was trying her very hardest.

"There she is," said Mrs. Muckle. "You must be my second pupil."

"I'm almost done," said Sugar. "Listen to this." She boldly played what she had learned, and just laughed when she made mistakes. "I have practicing to do."

"Good job," said Bailey. She really was very proud of her grandmother.

To their surprise, Mrs. Muckle did have gummed stars with her and put a silver one next to Sugar's name on the music page.

Sugar took a bow and said, "I need to make a phone call."

Bailey slid onto the piano bench and placed her hands on the keys. She loved the way the ivory felt, cool and smooth to the touch.

Mrs. Muckle said, "You do have good long fingers for playing. Let's get started."

Their teacher showed her how to form simple chords with her left hand as she played the tune with her right. Mrs. Muckle also taught Bailey finger patterns for a C scale. She wrote down what Bailey needed to practice in a notebook, on a page separate from Sugar's assignment. Bailey was happy that she also got a silver star.

"This will be enough for the first time," said Mrs. Muckle. "See you next week."

Bailey thought, *Wait till Norma Jean and my father see my piano.* She practiced her lessons until Sugar called her for supper.

35

Tending Sugar's Garden

"What are your plans for the evening?" asked Sugar.

"Reading, I guess," said Bailey, as she put the dishes in the cupboard. "I'm almost done with *The Secret Garden*. It is *so* good. I really like the part where they take Colin into the garden and he gets well."

"Me, too. But my garden isn't a secret. Everyone can see it, so before we get back to our books, I'll let you help me," said Sugar. "There is weeding and watering to be done."

Bailey had spent so much time with the Keswicks, she hadn't been to Sugar's garden in a while.

She was surprised to see that the corn was pushing up like blades of grass, and there were a few small round lumps on the tomato plants. The cucumber vine was growing in several directions, and her grandmother pointed to tiny cucumbers, like little green fingers.

Sugar showed Bailey how to pull the weeds so that the roots were removed. Some weeds came out easily, but Bailey needed to use a sharp trowel to dig out the others.

They put more straw around and under the strawberry plants to keep the berries from touching the ground and rotting. Bailey spotted three red berries. Sugar said it was okay to pick them. Bailey gave her the biggest one and ate the two smaller ones.

"Mmm," said Bailey. "These are the best ever."

"Let's hope we can harvest all of them before something else does."

"Something what?"

"Crows pecked my tomatoes last year, just as they were ripening. Thieves," said Sugar.

"We could make a scarecrow," said Bailey.

"Good idea," said Sugar. "I have some old clothes that we can stuff with straw. I'll put you in charge of making it."

Bailey said, "Maybe Emily can help. Guess what, Sugar? My favorite chapter in *The Secret Garden* is the one in which Colin discovers the magic in the garden. He likes to watch everything grow as he is learning to walk."

"I hope you will read that chapter to me later," said Sugar. "That is a magical one."

"Okay," said Bailey. "What's this?" She pointed to a long insect with large bent legs.

"That's a grasshopper," said Sugar. She touched it with a blade of grass and they watched it leap away.

Seeing the insect made Bailey think about her mother and the bug man. *Well, if Mom isn't coming back here, at least she will be surprised when I go see her,* thought Bailey. *She'll be so glad I came to visit that she'll forget about the bug man and it will just be us again.*

"A penny for your thoughts," said Sugar.

Bailey hadn't realized that she had been staring into space.

"Oh, nothing," she said. She didn't want to hurt her grandmother's feelings by telling her that she was still hoping to go live with her mother.

36

Detective Books

Sugar's recliner creaked as she leaned back and put her feet up in her library filled from floor to ceiling with books. She reached over to a table piled high with reading materials and selected one. Bailey curled up in a large overstuffed chair to finish the last chapters of *The Secret Garden*.

Secrets. Mysteries. Bailey thought about the thief at Keswick Inn. She looked around the room at all the books.

"Sugar," she said.

"Mmm," said her grandmother.

"Do you have any books about detectives or solving crimes?" asked Bailey, as she peered at the shelves.

Sugar put her book in her lap and said, "I believe I do—some for young people and some for adults. Your great-aunt Prudence, one of the family's fine wild women, studied law and then became a detective. She solved several important crimes."

"Really?" said Bailey.

"I have her books," said Sugar, as she creaked the recliner into its upright position and got up. "Let me see . . . ah, here they are." Sugar reached high on a shelf and pulled down several books. She handed them to Bailey.

"The kids' books are there. Nancy Drew, Hardy Boys. Freddie the Pig, and others," she said, pointing. "Here's one that I recently picked up on a treasure hunt. Help yourself."

Bailey selected several, including a tiny red-leather volume called *The World's Best 100 Detective Stories*. But it wasn't exactly what she had in mind. She reached for a few other titles and curled up again. Maybe she could learn how to set a trap to catch the thief. She opened a book with its jacket torn around the top. The cover pictured a detective smoking a pipe and holding a magnifying glass. The title was *How To Become a Really Good Detective* by Wally Sigafoose, Ph.D, detective emeritus, Sherlock Agency, Pittsburgh.

Bailey looked at the contents page. There were chapters on spying, what every detective needed to own, such as quiet shoes and a coat with big pockets, and how to catch the right person. Bailey decided to look at the last one first. Dr. Sigafoose wrote:

Don't be fooled. The first person you suspect may not be the real thief. Examine all the evidence carefully or you could make big mistakes.

Hmm, thought Bailey. She read further.

Pay attention to what is the same and what is different each time the crime is committed. Be observant.

How often had Sugar told her to be observant? Bailey decided to make a list of everything she could remember about the missing items when she went to her bedroom.

A lot were metal—different kinds of jewelry and coins. *It must have something to do with valuable metal objects,* thought Bailey. *The thief must be selling them to make money, so the thief is either just bad, or needs the money. It has to be someone who knows where the sorting room is.*

Bailey gave Sugar a good-night hug and kiss and went upstairs with the books and turned on her desk lamp.

She wrote down what was missing from the sorting room—the locket, watch, sock of coins—and who was in the house at the time. She could see why Noah thought Justin was the thief. He was always there when things were taken, and on two days he left early, right after new valuable treasures were placed in the sorting room. It didn't look good for him.

Bailey opened *London's Guide to Solving Crimes*. Chapter 5 contained exactly what she was looking for: "How to set a trap." *Wait till I tell Noah and Fred*, Bailey thought.

37

Confrontation

The sound of barking in the yard sent Sallie and Shadow to the top of a table where they could look out the window. It was Clover. She had followed the twins through the woods.

Fred yelled, "Give that back, you silly mutt!"

Clover had snatched a cleaning rag that was drying on Sugar's porch rail. The little dog, hoping that the boys would chase her, scurried just out of reach under the porch.

"I'll be ready in a minute," said Bailey.

"Be back after lunch," said Sugar. "We need to go shopping in Fredericksburg."

Bailey put the detective books in her knapsack and hurried after her friends.

When they reached the little graveyard halfway between their houses, Bailey called to the boys to stop for a minute. She told them what she had read and about her list.

"See," said Noah, "that proves it. It could only be Justin. Wait till he shows his face again."

Fred said, "But we don't have real proof. We need to set a trap. You said so yourself."

Noah stuck his chin out. "Whose side are you on?"

Bailey said, "It shouldn't be hard. If one more thing is missing, we just need to see who is there at the time. Here is what the book said about setting a trap." She showed them notes she had made from that chapter.

"That gives me an idea," said Noah. He reached in his jeans pockets and pulled out a little felt bag with a drawstring. In it was one of his most prized possessions—a pocketknife that had belonged to his birth father.

"I'm going to tell that creep, Justin, that I just found it in the attic and I'll put it on the sorting room table. We'll see how long it takes for him to steal it. We'll catch the thief and I'll get my knife back."

"What if he ditches the knife?" asked Fred.

"He won't," said Noah. "He'll want to keep it like all the rest of the stuff he stole."

~ ~ ~

Not long after Bailey and the twins signed in, Justin arrived. He barely glanced at the rest of the crew, but went straight up to Mr. Will for instructions. He would be helping Hayseed upstairs while the rest of them were to paint the room that would be Fred's. Miss Bekka had picked light green paint for three walls and plaid wallpaper for the fourth.

Clover bounded from room to room, looking for someone to play with her. Finally, she went to sleep in the hall.

When the adults were busy talking in the future school room, Noah saw his chance. Justin was in the hallway by himself.

"Hey, Justin," whispered Noah to him. "Look what I just found in the attic." He pulled little pouch out of his pocket and showed Justin the small silver pocketknife.

"It's a beauty," said Justin, slowly turning it over in his palm twice before handing it back.

"I'm going to put it in the sorting room," said Noah. "It will be safe there."

Noah returned to Bailey and Fred. "Easy as pie," he said.

Just as he had for several days, Justin said he had to leave early. While Justin was signing out and waiting to get paid, Noah quickly went to the sorting room.

"It worked," he said. "The knife is missing. Now, Mr. Justin Rudd will be missing, too."

He hurried down the stairs and ran out the door after Justin. Bailey and Fred, watching from the front porch, saw Noah try to grab Justin off his bike. "Give it back," he shouted. "You thief."

"I didn't take anything," yelled Justin angrily, giving Noah a shove. "Get away from me."

"You thief. Don't come back until you give everything back, you dirty rotten sneak," Noah shouted.

Justin raced away on his bike, with Ninja hurrying to keep up.

Noah, his face red with anger, returned to the porch.

"I hate him," he said. "And now he's got my father's knife."

"And we still don't have proof," said Fred, wiping his glasses on his shirt.

38

The Thief

Justin had not returned for more than a week. As Bailey signed her name in the log book, she realized that Justin had spent more time working than either the twins or she had.

She remembered how proud he was when Mr. Will showed them the shelves he made. She knew Norma Jean would want to know what had happened to him. The twins hadn't been joking around much since Noah had accused Justin of being the thief and Justin had gone off in anger. Bailey heard Miss Bekka's voice in the kitchen.

Miss Bekka's long hair was falling out of the clip she used to pin it up, and she had a yellow paint smudge on her cheek. She gave Bailey a big smile.

"I'm so glad you came today. The boys and their dad went to town to get more lumber. I could use help painting the bedroom at the top of the stairs."

"Sugar needs me back in the afternoon," said Bailey. "We're going on an adventure—a treasure hunt."

"Sugar's pretty special, isn't she," said Miss Bekka, motioning to Bailey to pick up the paint rollers and follow her.

Bailey nodded yes.

"Do you have any idea of what happened to Justin?" asked Miss Bekka as she rolled the sunny yellow paint on the wall. "It's odd that he hasn't been coming over for quite a while. That boy is such a good worker."

Bailey didn't want to tell a lie, but she also didn't think she should rat on Noah. All she could think of saying was, "He helps his mom a lot." It was true, but she knew it wasn't the reason that he had given up a job that paid good money.

Clover bounded into the room and grabbed Miss Bekka's paint rag. The moppy dog shook the rag as Miss Bekka laughed and said, "Give it back. Drop it." To both their surprise, Clover dropped the rag and sat down, looking like she wanted a game.

"I've never seen a dog that likes cloth so much," said Miss Bekka.

Bailey picked up the rag and hung it over a ladder rung.

Clover gave one last longing look at the cloth and padded out of the room. As Bailey rolled paint as high as she could reach around the door to the hall, she could see Clover sit and scratch her head with her back paw, then yawn, then walk into the sorting room.

Bailey put more paint on the roller and returned to the wall by the door.

Clover poked her head out of the sorting room.

What's that wacko dog got now? Bailey wondered.

When Clover didn't see anyone watching her, she dashed down the hall and down the stairs. Bailey realized that Clover had something in her mouth, something she had snatched from the sorting room table.

"What the . . . ," Bailey said out loud. She rushed to the window in time to see the white dog digging frantically under the lilac bush. Clods of dirt were flying. Clover placed the object in the hole and covered it over.

Bailey said excitedly, "Miss Bekka, I think I know what's been happening to all the missing things." Bailey put her paint roller in the tray and hurried down the stairs. Miss Bekka put her roller in the paint tray and quickly followed her.

Bailey rushed over to the lilac bush and used her hands to pull dirt away from the hole. She discovered that Clover had just buried the cloth doll that Noah found in the attic.

Bailey continued to dig in other spots where Clover had made holes. As she pulled off the soft dirt, she found the sock full of coins, and the little embroidered velvet bag with the silver locket, and the little pouch containing Noah's pocketknife.

"Wow!" said Bailey.

"Oh, my!" exclaimed Miss Bekka. "Let me get a shovel. I think the mystery of the thief has been solved by a very observant detective and wild woman, Miss Bailey Fish."

Clover put her head down on her paws as she watched Miss Bekka and Bailey uncover the rest of stolen treasures. Miss Bekka put them in a large basket and said she would make sure that Clover could not get into it. Then Miss Bekka said, "Before Clover got big enough to reach things on her own, I bet she climbed on a chair next to the sorting table to steal them."

"Everything is cloth," said Bailey, "or is wrapped in cloth. What a silly dog."

"Wait till we show Will and the boys," said Miss Bekka. "Who would have suspected the dog?"

Yeah, thought Bailey, glumly. *Now what will we do? Duh. Why didn't I put Clover on the list of suspects like Dr. Sigafoose said to do?*

She realized that somehow the triplets would have to make things right with Justin, and that wouldn't be easy.

39

Fred's Plan

"I've got something to show all of you," called Miss Bekka when her family returned.

Bailey watched Noah and Fred's faces as Miss Bekka revealed the contents of the basket and pointed out the thief. Clover wagged her tail proudly.

"Bailey deserves full credit for solving the mystery," said Miss Bekka. "Now we don't have to worry about a person taking our possessions."

Instead of looking overjoyed that the treasures were returned, Fred and Noah exchanged worried glances.

Finally Fred said, "Way cool, Bailey. Show us where you found the stuff."

"Back to work in ten minutes," said Mr. Will. "I need help unloading the truck."

Bailey led the way. She knew the boys just wanted to talk privately, especially about Justin.

"What are we going to do?" said Fred, when they reached the lilac bush.

"I dunno," said Noah.

"Justin has lost a lot of work time since you accused him," said Bailey, picking a leaf off the bush. "I know he needs the money to help his mother since his father is in jail. That's what Sugar said."

Noah took off his blue baseball cap and ran his fingers through his sticking-out hair.

The triplets were quiet, thinking. What could they possibly do to make things right?

"I guess we should tell Dad," Noah said. "You know he'll be mad at us. He'll want us to apologize to Justin and do something to make things up to him."

"What can we do?" asked Bailey. "Justin probably hates us."

Fred squatted down and brushed dirt back into the biggest hole. Then he took a stick and seemed to be tracing numbers in the dirt.

"Hey, Fred, what are you doing? We haven't got all day," said Noah.

His brother said, "I figure I've earned $35 so far toward my dirt bike. But my old bike will work a while longer."

Bailey quickly said, "I think I've made about $20. I don't need to go to Costa Rica right now."

Noah looked at both of them, and for the first time since the thief had been identified, he grinned. "I've earned about the same as Fred. I don't think I'll have time to make movies this summer. Triplet power," he said. "Let's go find Dad."

Mr. Will and Miss Bekka listened without interruption to Noah's story. Bailey was proud that he told the whole truth without trying to make himself look good. Noah admitted that he hadn't liked Justin, and that after he had seen the newspaper article about Justin's father getting arrested, he figured that Justin had to be the thief. Mr. Will scowled.

"You should have come to me or Mom," he said, "instead of taking matters into your own hands. Falsely accusing someone is wrong, son."

Noah looked away and shifted back and forth on his feet.

His father continued: "You know, it is also unfair to judge people by what their parents or other members of their family are like. And we shouldn't always judge people by what they have done in the past, because all of us can change. That doesn't mean you have to be best friends or even like someone—just be fair."

Miss Bekka added, "Treat them like you would want to be treated."

Noah looked at his hands. "I know. I know."

Mr. Will said, "And I'm not happy that you, Fred, and you, Bailey, didn't come to us, either. A great wrong has been done to that boy. How are we going to make it right?"

It was Fred's turn. "Bailey tried to stick up for Justin, but we didn't exactly believe her."

Bailey felt like her freckles were on fire and that she was as small as Clover.

The boys' father waited. Fred continued, "But, Dad, we have an idea. We want to give Justin all the money we have earned so far."

Mr. Will thought for a moment, then said, "That is a start, but more importantly, all of you need to apologize in person so that Justin knows you mean it and feels welcome to come back to work—if he is willing."

Noah swallowed hard. "Okay," he said.

Bailey knew the visit to the Rudds' was not going to be easy. She hoped Sugar would go with them, but first she would have to tell her grandmother what the triplets had done.

40

Apologies

Sugar had lunch ready when Bailey returned from the Keswicks' house. "Let's sit on the porch," said her grandmother, handing her a ham and cheese sandwich on rye bread. "It is such a beautiful day. Then we'll head out for our adventure. Besides, I have an announcement. Bruno just called and the developer has agreed to work with us to save the trees."

Normally Bailey would have been excited by the news, but she had Justin on her mind.

The entire time Bailey had been running home through the woods she tried to think of how she would tell Sugar, especially since the Keswicks wanted them all to be at the Rudds' house in an hour.

Bailey twisted her hair behind her ear and took a deep breath. "Sugar, can we go to the Rudds' first—I mean, on the way?"

Sugar looked surprised. "Sure, but whatever for?" she asked.

Bailey spilled out the whole story, including Noah's discovery of the newspaper article about the arrest of Justin's father.

Sugar pushed her glasses up on her nose and just when Bailey feared she would get a lecture, Sugar gave her a crinkly smile.

"That wasn't easy, was it? What have you learned from all of this?"

Bailey thought for a moment and said, "I should have stood up more for Justin, I guess."

"The hardest part will be to tell Justin you are sorry, in person," said Sugar.

~ ~ ~

Will Keswick had called ahead so Mrs. Rudd and the little girls were waiting for them on the front porch. Bailey did not see Justin or his dog. *What if he is hiding because he's afraid of us*? she wondered. Her heart was pounding. Justin had every right to be angry and so did his mother and Fern. Fern might not want to read with her any more.

Bailey looked at the twins. Noah had slicked his hair down, or tried to, and Fred had put on a clean soccer jersey. Noah had an envelope in his hand. Bailey knew it would have their work crew money in it.

"Mrs. Rudd, is Justin home?" asked Noah in a voice that was trying to be brave.

"Fern, go get your brother," said the mother. Fern ran around the side of the house calling his name.

"Would you like to sit down?" asked Mrs. Rudd.

"We can't stay long," said Sugar, "but we'll come back another day."

Where is Justin? Bailey wondered. *Why doesn't he come?* Something bit her ankle. She swatted and missed.

Fern reappeared. "He's coming," she said.

Justin walked around the side of the house with Ninja at his heels. Justin first looked alarmed at the sight of the boys, then glared at them.

Mr. Will nudged Noah, who took a step forward. "Justin," he said softly. His father nudged him again. "I'm . . . we're . . . very sorry that I said you were stealing things. That wasn't right. We were totally wrong. We want you to come back. Dad says you're the best worker ever," Noah said.

"I'm sorry, too," said Fred.

"It was mostly my fault," said Noah.

"I'm sorry, too," said Bailey. She looked at Justin's face. He was staring at them in disbelief.

"Clover was the thief," she said. "We just found out."

"The little dog?" Justin seemed as surprised as the rest of them had been. When Bailey finished telling how Clover buried the treasures, each wrapped in cloth, under the lilac bush, Justin actually smiled.

Mr. Will nudged Noah again. "Oh, here is something from the three of us, to try to make it up to you for the time you didn't come to work," said Noah. He handed Justin the envelope.

"I can't," said Justin, looking inside the envelope. "I don't want your money."

"Please, Justin," said Miss Bekka. "We do want you to come back to work at Keswick Inn as soon as you can."

Justin opened the envelope again, looked hard at Noah, Fred, and Bailey, and then at his mother. She said, "It's up to you. I really think they are sorry."

"Well, okay," he said, "but, some days I may need to leave early to babysit. Mom's got a job at a restaurant now."

So that was why he hurried off early at times. Bailey felt bad that she hadn't thought of that. *All this time Justin was helping his family. Boy, had they been really wrong about him.*

Justin handed his mother the envelope and appeared to be thinking as he turned to Noah and Fred. "Would you like to see Chuck the crow? You can feed him some corn."

"We all would," said Mr. Will.

Fern grabbed Bailey's hand as they followed Justin to the barn. Bailey heard Mr. Will offer to help make repairs to the Rudds' back porch.

"We've got a good work crew," he said.

"I don't know what to say," said Justin's mother.

"Just say yes," said Miss Bekka warmly. "That's what neighbors are for."

~ ~ ~

"Does he bite?" asked Noah as Justin put Chuck on his arm.

"Not usually," said Justin. "He pecks sometimes, but it doesn't hurt."

"I heard that crows steal things," said Fred.

"They like shiny objects," said Fern. "Chucky tried to take my necklace once while I was wearing it. And a piece of tin foil."

"Crows are very smart," said Justin, placing Chuck on Fred's arm. Fred held a kernel of corn in his open palm. Chuck quickly took it in his beak.

Justin showed them the shed where he made things.

"I'm glad I have you working for me," said Mr. Will. "You have a lot of talent."

Justin seemed embarrassed by the praise.

"Dad always said he was stupid," said Fern.

"I hope Justin knows he isn't," said Mr. Will. "Now let me have a turn with the crow."

41

Catching Dreams

"Everyone seemed to be impressed with Chuck," said Sugar, as she and Bailey followed signs for a yard sale in Spotsylvania Courthouse. Sugar hoped the picnic table that had been advertised in the paper hadn't been sold before they got there.

"Yeah," said Bailey. "I think Justin was surprised when Mr. Will asked if he would help train Clover since he is so good with animals."

"Justin does seem to have a way with them," said Sugar. "Look at how Ninja and Chuck respond to his commands. It's just like Dickon tames animals in *The Secret Garden*."

"Clover sure does need training. She's pretty wild," said Bailey. "She minds only when she feels like it."

"There is something I'd like to ask you about," said Sugar, pushing her glasses higher on her nose, as they turned left on Blockhouse Road. "I understand from Miss Bekka you were saving money to go to Costa Rica. How come you didn't tell me that?" Sugar looked at Bailey, who was staring out the truck window at the fields that were turning green.

Bailey said, "I was going to. It was just an idea, though. Noah and Fred wanted to know what I would save my money for and I just said 'Costa Rica.' It doesn't matter. Mom's busy with her book and the bug man, anyway."

Sugar said, "It might work out for you to visit there sometime, if that's what you and your mom would like. In fact, save your money from the Keswicks, and I'll give you extra jobs. We can open a bank account for you. And we can talk to your mom about helping pay for the trip, too." Sugar glanced at Bailey, who looked sad.

Bailey thought for a moment, then said, "I'll save enough so that you can go with me, Sugar. It would be more fun that way."

"What an adventure we wild women would have!" said Sugar. "We'll study everything we can before we travel so that we can enjoy our trip all the more."

Bailey reached across the seat and gave her grandmother a long hug as the pickup stopped at the yard sale, right next to the redwood picnic table that her grandmother hoped to buy.

"And if we don't go—?" asked Bailey.

"There is nothing wrong with having grand plans," said Sugar. "In fact, the wild women always like to have travel plans. There are so many wonderful places to see in this country and around the world."

Bailey nodded.

"And here is something else. I was going to save it for your birthday, but I think you might like it now," said Sugar, hugging back. She opened her purse and pulled out a dream-catcher like the one Bailey had admired at the powwow.

"How did you know?" asked Bailey, hardly daring to believe she was holding a red web with feathers.

"Always have good dreams," said Sugar, with a crinkly smile.

Book Club Questions

1. How does Bailey feel about Miss Dolly's death? What does she e-mail to Norma Jean about the funeral? How is this death different from the death of her cat, Barker? Have you ever lost a relative or a pet? Write about how you found out about it. How did you honor that person or pet after they were gone? Who did you want to talk to in order to sort out your feelings?

2. The author picks names like Hayseed Muckle, Dr. Snorge-Swinson, Clover, and Ninja. How do the names fit these characters or not? If you were writing a story, what name would you give an evil character? What name would you give a loyal pet?

3. Do you know anyone who is homeschooled? Why do you think families choose to do that? Would you like it? What are the advantages or

disadvantages? Set up an interview with someone you know who is homeschooled. Prepare questions to ask him or her.

4. What are Justin's dreams for his money? Why does he work so hard? If you had $100, how would you spend it? How about $1,000?

5. Do you think Bailey is jealous of her mother's new friend, Dr. Snorge-Swinson? Give reasons for your answer.

6. Do you think Bailey has certain expectations for her mother's visit? What do you think she is hoping will happen? Pretend you are Bailey and write about a dream she has about her mother's visit where either everything is absolutely perfect or everything goes wrong. Let your imagination go wild—your idea does not have to follow what happens in the book.

7. People sometimes make up their minds about a situation when they do not have all the facts. Bailey and her two friends think Justin is to blame for the thefts. What makes them come to that conclusion is something called "circumstantial evidence." Have you ever blamed someone and later found out it was not his or her fault? Has anyone ever blamed you and you were really innocent? Write about it.

8. When we find out we have wronged or wrongly blamed someone, what should we do? What does Bailey decide to do? Whose idea is it? Would you do the same as Bailey?

9. How does Sugar react to Bailey and the boys telling the truth? Should she and Mr. Will ground them? If you were Sugar, what would the punishment be?

10. In a short story or novel, often a character learns something and changes as a result of things that happen in the story. Is this true for any of the characters in this book? Does Justin change? Do the opinions of the other children toward Justin change?

Web sites

Powhatans and other Virginia tribes

www.baylink.org/Mattaponi/

www.native-languages.org/powhatan_words.htm

www.geocities.com/bigorrin/powhatan_kids.htm

www.baylink.org/pamunkey/history.html

www.virginia.org/site/features.asp?FeatureID=18

www.lenapeprograms.info/Wisdom.htm

www.nmai.si.edu/

www.native-languages.org/dreamcatchers.htm

www.VITALVA.org

Costa Rican Insects and Volcanoes

www.interlog.com/rainfrst/wildlife.html

http://kostaryka.org/wulkany2489/

(Sites available as of press time. Author and publisher have no control over material on these sites or links to other Web sites.)

From Sugar's Bookshelves

Alice Yazzie's Year, Ramona Maher

Everyday Life of the North American Indian, John Manchip White

First People: The Early Indians of Virginia, Keith Egloff and Deborah Woodward

Freddy the Detective, Walter Brooks

How to Become a Detective, C. Samuel Campbell

Louisa County History, edited by Pattie Cooke

Pocahontas: Young Peacemaker, Leslie Grouse

Rainy's Powwow, Linda Theresa Raczek

The Bridges in Edinburgh, Michele Sobel Spirn

The Life of the Powhatan, Rebecca Sjonger and Bobbie Kalman

The Secret Garden, Frances Hodgson Burnett

The World's Best 100 Detective Stories, Eugene Thwing, editor-in-chief (1929)

Glossary

Adoption: To make someone else's child by birth legally your own. Parents might adopt children of relatives (like Noah), or through an adoption agency (like Fred).

Birth parents: The people to whom a child is born.

Boutique: A fancy, speciality store that might sell jewelry, clothes or shoes.

Calico: A cotton cloth with a pattern.

Calling hours: A time before a funeral when friends and family get together to show their respect for the person who died and talk about the person's life. People often cry, so there are boxes of tissue here and there. Usually there are lots of flowers and sometimes pictures of the person who died. Funerals, often the next day, are usually religious services.

Clear-cut: To remove all trees from the land.

Compost: A mixture of decayed leaves, grasses and sometimes household waste, such as lettuce, apple cores, and coffee grounds, that is used for fertilizing a garden.

Confederacy: Groups that band together to help each other out in war or peace.

Entomologist: A scientist who studies insects.

Fall Line: Where the waterfalls are located on a river—a natural geological division.

First People: The people who lived in what is now the United States before the white settlers arrived.

Jamestown: The first permanent English settlement (1607) in what is now the United States. The English fought with the Indians to gain control of the land.

Lattice: Strips that are laid across each other to create a checkerboard effect.

Molas: Artistic cloth sculptures made by Kuna Indian women of Panama. Molas often decorate clothing or are used as wall hangings.

Powwow: An American Indian social gathering, often with competitive dancing.

Piano tuning: Adjusting the pitch or sound of notes on the piano so that they are in perfect harmony.

Trail of Tears: From the 1820s to the 1840s, the U.S. government forced several tribes, including the Cherokees, Chickasaws, Choctaws, Creeks, and Seminoles, to move from their own lands to reservations west of the Mississippi River. The Native Americans were mistreated and many got sick and died.

Tulip tree: Also called the tulip poplar, this tree grows widely in North America. Its flowers are tulip-shaped and its wood is often used to make cabinets.

Upright piano: A type of piano with a high back that conceals the strings, unlike the grand piano that is flat like a table and takes up a lot of space.

Wounded Knee: U.S. soldiers killed more than 200 Sioux Indians in 1890 while the Native Americans were prisoners. Wounded Knee, South Dakota, is the name of the creek where the massacre occurred.

Zoning: Communities decide that certain areas will have different uses. Some zones are for business, some for houses, some for farming. When someone wants to put a shopping center in a farming or housing zone, they need to get permission from the zoning board to have the zoning changed.

Above: The beautiful feather and bead headdress of Chickahominy Chief Stephen Adkins.

Dancers from many tribes participate at a Chickahominy Powwow east of Richmond, Virginia.

Rachel and Emily Tupponce, age six, are triplets (their brother, Connor, is not pictured). The girls are jingle dancers at a powwow. See the cone-shaped jingles on their dresses. Their father, Reginald, is an Upper Mattaponi, and their mother, Dawn, is a Chickahominy.

Above: Pamunkey decorative pottery is displayed and for sale at a Chickahominy Powwow. The symbols on the pots tell stories.

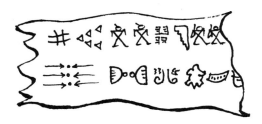

*The drawings on Sugar's orange-brown
pottery bowl tell the story of an agreement
made in 1646 between the Pamunkey
Indians and white settlers representing
King James of England. At Thanksgiving
time, when the geese are flying, the Indians
follow a trail to meet with the white men.
There they will smoke the peace pipe and
present furs and wild game and wish the
white men good luck.*

Historian Sandra Speiden's artifact collection includes cached or unfinished blades (left).

Below are spear points (larger than arrowheads) and an antler, which was used to flake the edges of projectile points found in Orange County, Virginia. Many were discovered on the Speiden's Springdale Farm or at 200 other sites in Orange, Madison and Greene counties. The antler is from modern times. Even smaller "arrowheads" could have been used as dart tips.

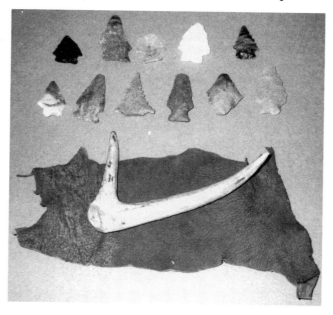

Above: Celts are sophisticated woodworking tools invented by the Middle Woodland People between 500 BC and 900 AD.

Below: These hammerstones were used for pounding by various Indian tribes. Celts and hammerstones were found in Orange County, Virginia.

INDIAN STONE AXE

DISCOVERED BY MR. WOOD
WHILE PLOWING AT HIS HOME
ACROSS FROM BEREA CHURCH
ON SOUTH ANNA RIVER.

SOURCE: MR. CHARLES W. WOOD
07.19

The axes and arrowheads (projectile points) were found in Louisa County. They are believed to have been used by Monacans. They, and other Indian artifacts, including grinding stones, are on display in the Louisa County Museum in Louisa, Virginia, and were photographed courtesy of the museum.

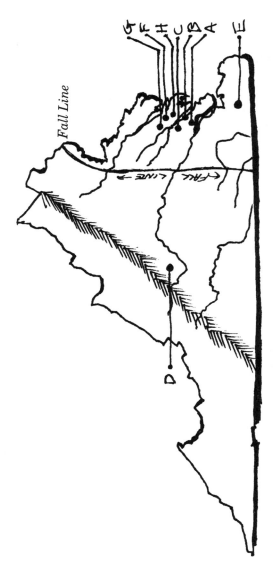

Indian Tribes Recognized by the State of Virginia—A. Chickahominy Tribe; B. Chickahominy Tribe—Eastern Division; C. Mattaponi Tribe; D. Monacan Indian Nation; E. Nansemond Tribe; F. Pamunkey Tribe; G. Rappahannock Tribe; H. Upper Mattaponi Tribe. The Blue Ridge Mountains are represented by feathery line at left; The Fall Line, by solid line toward right.

Acknowledgments

Thank you to everyone who has offered encouragement, ideas, information and suggestions for this book, but especially to Jim Salisbury; Nancy Bailey Miller, for developing discussion questions; Abbie Grotke; Pamela Gastineau; Reginald Tupponce, a member of the Upper Mattaponi and president of the Virginia Indian Tribal Alliance for Life; historian Pattie Cooke, curator of the Louisa County Museum; archeologist and historian Sandra Speiden and her family members; Christopher Grotke; students in the Orange County School District; Hallie Vaughan; Bert and Barbara Stafford and David Black. I am grateful for special inspiration from Jake Wettlaufer, who always greeted us with a wagging tail and cloth in his mouth; and from Amber Freidel.

About the Author

 Linda Salisbury draws her inspiration for the Bailey Fish series from her experiences in Florida and Central Virginia, and from those as a mother, mentor, former foster mother, and grandmother.

She is a former newspaper editor and columnist, who writes children's book reviews and articles for various publications. She is the author of six other books.

She enjoys boating on Lake Anna with her husband, Jim. They share their home with five lazy cats.

About the Artist

Artist Christopher Grotke of Brattleboro, Vermont, is the creative director for MuseArts, Inc. He is an award-winning animator and has been featured in a number of publications, including the *Washington Post* and *New York Times,* and his work has been seen on PBS's "The Creative Spirit."

He has done illustrations and drawings for eight books. He has one adventurous cat who likes to hike in the woods with him. Visit his Web site at www.musearts.com.